Friends 'Til the End

ReShonda Tate Billingsley

Pocket Books

New York   London   Toronto   Sydney

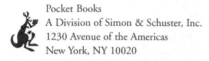

Pocket Books
A Division of Simon & Schuster, Inc.
1230 Avenue of the Americas
New York, NY 10020

First Pocket Books trade paperback edition February 2009

POCKET and colophon are registered trademarks of Simon & Schuster, Inc.

For information about special discounts for bulk purchases, please contact Simon & Schuster Special Sales at 1-800-456-6798 or business@simonandschuster.com

Manufactured in the United States of America

10 9 8 7 6 5 4 3 2 1

Library of Congress Cataloging-in-Publication Data

Billingsley, ReShonda Tate.
    Friends 'til the end / ReShonda Tate Billingsley.
        p. cm.
    Summary: When sixteen-year-old Jasmine gets permission to date C.J., their relationship blooms until a gang sets one of their brothers against the other, leading to problems that require faith, hope, and support from the Good Girlz after-school church group.
    [1. Dating (Social customs)—Fiction. 2. Gangs—Fiction. 3. Friendship—Fiction. 4. High schools—Fiction. 5. Schools—Fiction. 6. African Americans—Fiction. 7. Mexican Americans—Fiction. 8. Christian life—Fiction.] I. Title. II. Title: Friends 'til the end.
    PZ7.B4988Fri 2009
    [Fic]—dc22

                                                                    2008033077

ISBN-13: 978-1-4165-5877-4
ISBN-10:   1-4165-5877-2

**Good Girlz
Series**

Friends 'Til
the End

Other titles in the Good Girlz series

Fair-Weather Friends
Getting Even
With Friends Like These
Blessings in Disguise
Nothing But Drama

Also by ReShonda Tate Billingsley

Can I Get a Witness?
The Pastor's Wife
Everybody Say Amen
I Know I've Been Changed
Let the Church Say Amen
My Brother's Keeper
Have a Little Faith
(with Jacquelin Thomas, J. D. Mason, and Sandra Kitt)

To the librarians and teachers who continue
to ignite a love of reading.

A Note from the Author

Here I am on book number six in the Good Girlz series and I still have to pinch myself and ask, "Is this for real?"

It is. The success of the Good Girlz proves God truly is in the blessing business. See, when I started I just wanted to find a happy medium in teen reading. I wanted to write quality, page-turning books that would ignite a love of reading in young people. I'm honored to say that not only has that flame been lit, but it's burning out of control. And in this era of advanced technology—MP3 players, iPods, YouTube, MySpace, and 763,487,999 katrillion cable channels—it's refreshing to see young people still excited to pick up a book.

I am especially excited to see the Good Girlz in good

company on the shelves. Of course, much love to Stephanie Perry Moore, who started the whole journey of telling good, clean Christian stories for young people. But I must also say, if you haven't already, please check out young adult books by some of my favorite authors: Jacquelin Thomas, Victoria Christopher Murray, and Michelle Stimpson.

I love me some exciting, drama-filled adult books, but they're just that—for adults. Our young people now have clean, quality fiction. Let's make sure they're reading it.

Thank you to the thousands of young people who have read, and will read, my books. Thank you to the parents, teachers, librarians, and concerned adults who are putting these books in their hands. Your efforts are making a difference. Just ask the young lady who emailed me recently about how she has gone from hating reading to reading every young adult book she can find (especially the ones that mirror her world). Or ask the gang member (yes, you heard me right, gang member) I met at a book signing, who was given a book, decided to read it, then emailed me to find out "what was going to happen next." As the commercial says, the books: $10. Moments like that: Priceless.

So thank you one more time. You are the fuel that keeps my fire burning.

Much love,
ReShonda

P.S.—Check me out on Myspace at www.myspace.com/goodgirlz1 and at www.goodgirlz1.org.

Friends 'Til the End

1

Jasmine

Different day, same drama. Me and two of my best friends, Camille and Angel, were just leaving our history class when we noticed a commotion in the hallway.

"What's going on?" Camille asked, standing on her tiptoes trying to see over the crowd of students. Camille Harris was the nosiest person I'd ever met, which was why I thought she'd chosen the perfect career to pursue—news reporter.

I shrugged. "Your guess is as good as mine. It's probably just another fight, or some girl goin' off because her boyfriend was talking to another girl. Who knows? Who cares?" I never was one to be all up in someone's business, and I wasn't about to start now. Until I met Camille,

Angel, and our other best friend, Alexis (who went to a different school), I really kinda kept to myself. I'll admit it, I'm not the friendliest person on the face of the earth, but after you spend your life getting teased and talked about because of your size (I am supertall and thick—not fat, but thick), then you just start to keep your distance from two-faced girls.

But the Good Girlz changed all of that for me. The Good Girlz is a group that was started over a year and a half ago by Rachel Jackson Adams, the first lady of Zion Hill Missionary Baptist Church. She started the group here in Houston as part of a church youth outreach program. Miss Rachel gave us that name because she said she wants us to always "strive for the good things in life." I know the name makes people think we're all goody-goody, but trust, we are so far from that. Camille is always getting in trouble behind some boy. Angel is a teenage mom. Alexis was the loneliest rich girl I'd ever met. And I had trouble with my temper. Our lives are nothing but drama, but we've been growing and, I'd like to think, learning a thing or two, which was why I had no interest in the mess brewing in the hallway.

"Is that your locker everybody is standing in front of?" Angel asked, bringing me out of my thoughts. I peered closer. Last week somebody vandalized a bunch of school lockers. I hoped they hadn't gotten to mine, especially because I had my brother's MP3 player in there and he would kill me if something happened to it.

Since I was close to six feet tall—and one of the tallest girls in the eleventh grade—I could easily see over the commotion. The crowd was gathered right in front of my locker, staring and pointing. One of the lockers next to mine was empty, but maybe they were looking at something in Daysia's locker, which was on the other side. Daysia was always caught up in some mess, so it wouldn't surprise me if somebody had tagged her locker.

I began making my way through the crowd. "That's my locker," I said, pushing my way past everyone. Camille and Angel were close on my heels.

I braced myself. I still wasn't the most-liked person around school, so it very well could've been someone writing some mess about me.

"Dang, that has got to be the biggest basket I've ever seen!" Camille said as we stopped in front of my locker.

My mouth was on the floor at the sight of the huge candy bouquet and gift basket sitting there, with a big banner that said FOR JASMINE JONES. Camille had her nose all up in the basket.

"Girl, look at these chocolate-covered strawberries. Dang!" Camille exclaimed once again, reaching inside the basket. "And is that an iPod?"

"Who is it from?" Angel asked. "And why in the world would they leave all this stuff out here for somebody to steal?"

A small smile crept onto my face as I thought about my complaints yesterday about not having an iPod.

"Who do you think it's from?" Camille snapped, pulling a box of perfume out of the basket. She turned back to me and grinned widely as she sprayed perfume on her neck. "It's from her boo."

My smile grew wider. My boo. C.J. Taylor definitely knew how to treat a girl. I knew he was planning something nice for Valentine's Day, but I had no idea he was gonna go all out like this.

I casually glanced over my shoulder at Tori and some other cheerleaders who were standing around, staring at my basket.

Tori—who hated my guts for no other reason than the fact that she was just a hater—would never give me my props. But when I looked at the little dried-up carnation she held in her hand, she didn't have to say a word. I knew she was sick with jealousy.

"Oh, there's a card," Angel said, pointing inside the basket.

I reached for it, but Camille beat me to it.

"Oooooh, let's see what C.J. has to say," she said, snatching the card out.

I playfully rolled my eyes. Normally, I would've been embarrassed and jerked the card back and gone somewhere to read it in private. But when I tell you I really don't like Tori, I mean that. So I took a lot of pleasure in letting Camille read the card out loud, especially because of the growing crowd.

Tori stood back off to the side trying to act like she wasn't interested, but I knew she could hear. And even if she couldn't, her girls were goin' to go back and tell her.

" 'To the most beautiful girl at Madison High School, no, make that in the world,' " Camille began reading. "Now, what is he writing about me for?" she joked.

I laughed and reached for the card. "Give it here."

"Okay, okay," she said, pulling it out of my reach. "I'll finish. 'I was wandering around knowing something wasn't quite right. Then I figured out what had been missing when you came into my life. My life wasn't complete, this much is true. My life wasn't complete because I was missing you. Happy Valentine's Day.' "

"Awwww," several people around us said at the same time.

"Man, that's some corny stuff!" a boy yelled from the back. Several girls turned around and shot him evil eyes.

"That's why you don't have a girlfriend now," some girl snapped at him.

"That is so sweet," this girl named Zinetta said, also trying to sneak a look in my basket. "Is that from C.J.?"

"Yeah, it is," I said, taking the card from Camille.

Zinetta's boyfriend was standing next to her holding a single balloon with a ribbon. She looked at him and cut her eyes.

"What?" he said, frowning up. "Everybody can't be Rico Suave. That's some old busta stuff anyway."

Zinetta huffed and stomped off with her boyfriend close behind her.

"If you all would excuse me," I said, leaning down to pick up my basket. It was really heavy. I couldn't wait to get it home and go through every single item.

I said my good-byes, then walked toward the football field where I knew C.J. would be practicing. I loved the fact that he would do sweet stuff like this and not care about anybody riding him. With C.J., if he was feeling it, he would do it, and unlike most boys his age, he couldn't care less what anyone had to say about it.

I stood back and watched him as he darted around, over, and across anyone trying to tackle him.

C.J. was a thin guy, but he had supernatural speed. He was a senior but looked like a professional football player as he ducked one guy, jumped over another, and left some player in his dust as he headed toward the goal line. He was an all-around superstar athlete, starring on both the football and the basketball teams.

I sat down on the bleachers and waited for him to finish practice. He saw me and blew me a kiss. I blew one back.

It's hard to believe that a dude has my nose wide open. Of me and my friends, Camille is the boy-crazy one. She's the one who spends every waking moment thinking about boys. Shoot, her Myspace ID is Boycrazy. My other best friend and fellow Good Girl, Alexis, is boy-crazy, too, although not to the extreme Camille is. Angel, the fourth member of our clique, is a little bit more reserved. But it's nothing for a cute guy to turn her head.

Me, on the other hand, I'm not trying to hear nothing about no dude. Or let me rephrase that, I didn't use to be trying to hear nothing. I know I'm sixteen and all, but I didn't even start liking boys until last year. That's when I hooked up with my first boyfriend—Donovan.

Donovan is the only other boy that has been able to get in my head. He played basketball at my school before heading to the University of Texas at Austin to play there. I know it might not seem like it, but I'm not into athletes.

Just like C.J., Donovan pursued me. Then he dropped me like some hot fries when he got to college.

C.J. had been a pain in my behind since middle school, when he used to call me Grape Ape because I'm so tall and thick. And he was a little scrawny something. But C.J. must've prayed really hard, worked out, or something, because he came back from summer vacation this year a good foot taller, filled out, and actually looking pretty cute. He had smooth, dark skin, a close-cropped fade, and the most perfect white teeth I'd ever seen.

I didn't want to give C.J. the time of day at first, but he wore me down and got me to give him my phone number. We started talking and I haven't looked back since.

"Hey, baby," he said, racing off the football field. "I see you got your Valentine's Day gift." He removed his helmet and dropped his backpack, which he'd stopped to pick up on his way over to me.

"I did," I said, leaning in and quickly kissing him on the cheek. "But I can't believe you just left it sitting by my locker. Anybody could've taken it."

"Trust, somebody was watching it. My boy Spencer would've been right there if anybody had dared touch it."

"Well, thank you." I glanced at the basket. "I can't believe you got me an iPod."

C.J. had a part-time job at his uncle's construction company and I know his family had a little money, but I definitely never would've guessed he had it like that.

"You deserve it. Sorry it's the small one. But my paycheck wasn't what I thought it would be."

"Please, it's bigger than the invisible one I have right

now." C.J. and I had been together only two months, but I was so into him, I didn't even mind his dripping nasty sweat on me.

"Happy Valentine's Day," he said.

"Same to you. You know you tripped out with this big ol' basket." I squeezed the big bouquet. I felt bad because I'd gotten him only a card. I made a mental note to see if Alexis would loan me some money so I could go buy him something after school, because as usual, I was beyond broke.

"You know how I do it," C.J. said, taking a seat next to me. "Nothing but the best for my baby."

I blushed. "I told you, you didn't have to go overboard like this."

"Then I guess you don't want part two of your Valentine's Day gift." He pulled a small box out of his backpack and held it up.

"Yes, I do," I said, happily snatching the box from him. I had been dead broke all my life, and I wasn't used to nice things. So although I didn't want to seem like some money-hungry chick, I absolutely loved getting gifts from C.J.

He grinned as I tore open the package. Inside was the prettiest bracelet I'd ever seen. It was sterling silver and had a cross dangling from it.

"Oh, my God. This is tight!" I said, holding it up. But I quickly lost my enthusiasm. "Where in the world am I supposed to tell my mom all this stuff came from?"

"Tell her it came from your man," he said boastfully.

"Yeah, right." I laughed. "Let me try walking in my

house talking 'bout, 'Oh, Mama, look at my iPod and bracelet my man bought.' I don't think so." My mama didn't play that. She and my grandmother were old school. They didn't even let me talk on the phone with boys until recently. But I'd been wearing my mom down, trying to get her to let me start going out on my own with C.J., and I had a feeling she was about to give in.

"So, am I still coming over for dinner tonight?" C.J. asked.

"Yep. My mom wants to meet you before she decides if she's going to let us go out."

He jumped up. "Let me go clean up. I'll see you at your house at six thirty."

I smiled and waved good-bye. C.J. coming to my house to meet my mom. I never would've thought I'd see the day. But I also never would have thought I'd be feeling someone like I was feeling him.

I said a quick prayer. "Lord, please don't let any drama go down with my mama," I whispered. I had a good feeling about C.J. and me, and I definitely didn't need any drama messing it up.

2

Jasmine

I nestled the phone between my ear and shoulder as I held up yet another outfit and looked at it in the mirror.

"Girl, I am so nervous," I said, my voice shaking. This would be the fourth outfit I'd tried on, but nothing seemed right for my first "official date." I'd been on dates before, but this was the first time I had my mother's blessings. "My mama has never wanted to meet one of my boyfriends," I continued.

"You ain't had but two," Camille cracked.

My relationship with my mother was strained at times. She wasn't the most loving person on earth, but lately, I'd learned that she loved me the way she knew how. Even though she wasn't all touchy-feely, she worked two jobs and tried to give us the best life possible. To her that was a sign of love. I was just happy that me and my mom were getting to the point where we could even talk about boys.

"Anyway, my mom has never wanted to meet a boy, period," I continued. "And she sure has never even thought about letting me leave the house with one. I am seriously trippin'." I sighed, deciding on the brown Apple Bottoms shirt and jeans, one of the few name-brand outfits I owned.

I'd been on the phone with Camille for almost an hour, and she hadn't managed to calm me down at all. C.J. would be here any minute. I was so nervous, my palms were sweating and I was getting a headache. Camille was in the middle of telling me that I was making a big deal out of nothing when I heard the doorbell ring. Before I could hang up the phone, I heard my older sister Nikki yelling down the hall.

"Jasminium Nichelle Solé Jones, your little boyfriend is here," Nikki taunted. I swear I couldn't stand that girl sometimes. Almost as much as I couldn't stand that stupid name I was born with.

"Stop calling me that," I said when I walked out of the room I shared with her. "You know I hate that name. I hope you don't call yourself trying to embarrass me in front of my company. For your information, he already knows my real name."

Nikki rolled her neck at me. "I bet I could tell him some stuff about you I'm sure he doesn't know. Like how you used to eat boogers when you were a little girl."

My sister really and truly made me sick. That happened *one* time. When I was, like, five and she hadn't let me live it down.

Before I could go off on her, my grandmother came in the room wearing a flowered apron and smelling like chicken grease.

"That's enough, girls. Y'all get on my nerves with all that fighting. You better shut up before I make you hug each other right here in the middle of this living room."

I looked at my grandmother in horror. That's how my granny tortures us when we fight. She knows how much we hate to hug. Once she made us stand and hug each other for fifteen minutes straight. Fighting between siblings wasn't allowed in my house and that was a hard rule to follow, seeing as how I had three younger brothers in addition to Nikki. Jaquan was just one year younger than me. Jaheim was eleven and Jalen was six. All of us lived in this small three-bedroom apartment, with me and Nikki in one room, my brothers in another, and my mom and grandmother in the last room.

C.J. was still standing by the door with a smile on his face, waiting on someone to invite him into the room. My grandmother walked over to him and shook his hand.

"I'm sorry about that, baby. Them grandchildren of mine don't have no manners. All they do is fight." I was surprised she was being so nice, especially considering the fact that she didn't want me to date yet. If she had her way, I'd be twenty-seven before I went on my first date.

"I'm Jasmine's grandma," she continued. "And you must be C.J.? And what's yo' real name? 'Cuz I know your mama ain't named you no C.J."

"No, ma'am." C.J. chuckled. "My real name is Calvin Jr. It's nice to finally meet you. And believe me, I understand about fighting with your sister. I have a very overprotective twin sister at home that I fight with every now and then. But we can never stay mad for too long. We're pretty close. It's just me, her, and my brother, and I wouldn't trade my family for anything."

Good answer, I thought.

"Mmmmm," C.J. said, sniffing the air. "Is that fried chicken I smell? It smells better than Popeye's."

My heart fluttered as I watched C.J. work his charm on my grandmother. I was grinning from ear to ear as I gazed at my boyfriend standing there looking handsome in his khaki pants, yellow tie, and sweater vest. My grandmother was looking him up and down, smiling with approval. She laughed. "Boy, Popeye's ain't no real chicken. Make yourself comfortable, dinner's almost ready."

I wanted to reach out and give C.J. a nice long hug but I knew my grandmother wasn't having that. So I settled for sitting on the opposite end of the couch from him. We were laughing and joking about something that happened at school earlier in the week when my mom came in the door with my brother Jaquan, who she'd just picked up from basketball practice. She had a bag of groceries in her hand.

As she entered, C.J. rose to his feet. "It's nice to meet you, Ms. Jones. Can I help you with that bag?" he asked.

"Such a polite young man. You must be the C.J. I keep hearing my daughter talk so much about," my mom said as she handed C.J. the bag. "My son is getting the rest of the groceries out of the car, but you can take this one into the kitchen."

My mom nodded her approval at me as C.J. walked into the kitchen. "He's cute," she mouthed.

Just as C.J. was coming back into the room, Jaquan sauntered into the house balancing three or four bags in his arms. I was even more nervous about Jaquan giving me a hard time about C.J. than I was about my mom meeting him.

Jaquan and I had never seen eye to eye on anything, but lately we had really been getting along. I guess because he was finally growing up and not being so immature all the time. I actually kind of valued his opinion, so it was important to me that he and C.J. got along. They knew each other from school but were not really friends. Jaquan was only a sophomore, but everybody knew who he was because several top colleges were already scouting him for a basketball scholarship.

"What's up?" Jaquan mumbled. He gave C.J. a nod as he passed him on his way to the kitchen.

"You need some help, man?"

"Naw, dog, I got it," my brother replied. "Plus, my triflin' little brothers need to get the rest of the bags."

Jaquan wasn't much of a talker, at least not to people he didn't really deal with, so I was a little surprised C.J. even got that much conversation out of him.

"Jaheim, Jalen, get your butts out here and help with the bags," my mom screamed down the hall.

My younger siblings had been holed up in their room

playing video games and were not happy about having to stop the game.

Jaheim stomped out of the room, pouting, and said, "Why we always gotta do all the work? It's not fair!"

"Boy, do you want eat? You don't work, you don't eat!" my mom fussed and popped him on the back of his head as he passed her. "And if you sass me again, I'm going to knock your teeth out your mouth."

"Aww, man," Jaheim said as he stomped toward the door. Nikki stuck her foot out and purposely tripped him. He got up and charged at her. But she quickly stopped him by pushing him to the floor.

"Go on, little squirt," she said.

He started crying as he tried to pull himself up again.

"Would you two stop it?" my mom chastised.

As usual, I was mortified at my family's behavior. I looked at C.J. and was about to apologize on their behalf, but before I could say anything, C.J. looked at me and said, "Jasmine, your family is too funny. I really like them."

Leave it to my baby to be so understanding. That's why I liked him so much. He and his family had so much, but he was never the type to judge others. I'd been nervous about his coming to our apartment because it was small and definitely wasn't in the nicest of neighborhoods, but he didn't seem fazed at all.

C.J. stayed through dinner, and the rest of the evening went off without any more problems. C.J. and Jaquan talked a lot about basketball and who was who in the NBA. I could tell that my mom and grandmother were impressed with C.J., especially after he told them he sang in his church's choir. They kept smiling all throughout dinner and nodding their heads. Even my pesky little brothers were on their best behavior the rest of the evening. So far, I was very pleased with the way the whole evening was going. I couldn't wait to call Alexis, Camille, and Angel and tell them all about it.

By the time C.J. left, it was too late to call my girls and tell them about my night. I couldn't use the phone after nine, and I didn't want to give my mom any reason to start trippin'. I guess it would just have to wait until the morning.

I was in my room putting on my pajamas when Mama came in.

"Jasmine, I really like your little boyfriend. He seems like a good kid," she said, leaning against the door frame.

"He is, Mama," I said apprehensively. This whole mother-daughter bonding thing was new to me, so I didn't really know how to take it.

She looked at me. "I never thought I would hear myself saying this, but I guess you are finally growing up. If you have to have a boyfriend, at least I can say you made a good choice. I love you and I'm proud that I raised you to make good choices."

Astonished doesn't even begin to describe my feelings after Mama said that. I was speechless. Don't get me wrong, I knew my mother loved me, I just never in a million years thought I'd ever hear her say something like that.

"I know this is all catching you by surprise," my mother continued. "I don't get to say that too often. Now that you are sixteen and really interested in boys, I have to accept you're not my baby anymore. Honestly, there was a part of me that liked the tomboyish side of you because I was hoping it would keep you away from boys. But I love the young lady you're becoming. You have matured a lot over the past few months. I guess I'm saying all of this to say, it would be okay for you and C.J. to go to the movies or something."

"Yes!" I screamed as I jumped up to hug my mother. This was a day I never thought would come. And it had to be the happiest day of my life.

3

Angel

I looked over at Jasmine and started laughing. I had never seen my girl sweat so much. We were on our way to C.J.'s house to pick him up to go to the movies. Out of all the days for his car to break down, it had to be this morning. Luckily, my sister, Rosario, had allowed me to use her car for the day in exchange for my agreeing to watch her kids while she and her boyfriend went out the next night. I still don't know how I ended up playing chauffeur, but my mom had my eighteen-month-old daughter, Angelica, and I welcomed any excuse to get out of the house. So when Jasmine told me she and C.J. had to cancel their date because his car broke down, I offered to drive.

"Girl, what is wrong with you?" I asked, carefully

changing lanes. "You look like you are about to throw up." Jasmine shot me a dirty look but didn't respond. "All I know is, you better not throw up in my sister's car," I warned, only half joking. Rosario, who was eight years older than me, drove a Toyota Corolla, but you would've thought it was a Benz the way she took care of it.

"I'm okay. Just a little nervous. I have never met a guy's family before." Jasmine sat in the passenger seat biting her nails as we pulled up in front of the house. "I hope they like me," she said nervously. "Do I look okay?"

"You look great, girl. Quit trippin'," I said. "As long as you keep the smart comments to yourself, you will be fine."

Jasmine had a bad habit of going off, especially when somebody gave her a hard time, and I was sure C.J.'s twin sister, Cynthia, was going to have something smart to say. Cynthia had a reputation for being a little strong-minded and very protective of her twin brother.

It was just our luck. Cynthia answered the door and didn't look too happy.

Jasmine smiled politely and said, "Hey, Cynthia. Is C.J. home?"

"Yeah," she said, before turning and walking off. "C.J.," she yelled. Jasmine and I exchanged glances, wondering if we were supposed to follow her in. Cynthia stopped and spun back toward us. "Y'all just gon' stand outside?"

We quickly walked inside. Cynthia made her way toward the back of the house.

As we stood in the foyer and looked into the living room, I was in awe of how beautiful C.J.'s home was. It was decorated like something out of a fancy home-and-garden magazine. The sofa and matching love seats were covered with a floral print. There were huge ceramic vases that were taller than me in the corners of the room. Hanging on the walls were the most gorgeous pieces of artwork I had ever seen. Everything in the room just seemed to flow, and the room looked very tidy, like no one ever even went in it.

I followed Jasmine into the room and had a seat on the couch. As soon as we sat down, C.J.'s mom and dad came in and greeted us.

"Well, hello. You must be Jasmine. I feel like I know you already the way my son talks about you all the time," his mom said. "And who must this be?" she asked, referring to me.

Jasmine stood up. "It's nice to meet you, Mr. and Mrs. Taylor. This is my friend Angel. She's giving us a ride."

I saw Mr. Taylor frown up, but his wife stuck her hand out to shake mine. "It's nice to meet you, Angel. C.J. will be out in a minute," she told me.

The Taylors sat down and talked with us for a while until C.J. was ready. I was surprised at how Jasmine managed to turn on the charm. You never would have known that ten minutes ago she was on the verge of losing it. I was actually impressed with my girl.

C.J.'s mom was smiling from ear to ear as she listened to Jasmine tell her about her plans to go to college. Some of the future plans Jasmine talked about, even I didn't know. And we tell each other everything. I wondered if she was just making up some of that stuff to get on his parents' good side. I was definitely going to have to remember to ask Jasmine about it later.

C.J. and his younger brother, Al, came down the stairs. I knew C.J. had a brother who went to a different school, but I had never met him. He had cute light brown eyes, but he was short, probably five-five or so, and he was nowhere near as cute as C.J. He did have a roughness about him that was very attractive. He had on baggy, sagging pants and a wife-beater tank top. He looked to be the total opposite of C.J., who was dressed like Kanye West in blue jeans and polo-style shirt.

C.J.'s dad's voice interrupted my thoughts.

"Boy, when you buying me my new Cadillac?"

"Huh?" Al asked.

"I said, when you buying me my new Caddy? Because you must be some big-shot rapper the way you dress."

"Awww, Dad, you trippin'," Al groaned.

"You gon' be trippin' . . . all over them pants. Pull those doggone jeans up and go put on a real shirt. Can't you see we've got company!"

"Dang, Daddy! Why you trippin'? This the style," Al argued.

"I got yo' style. Just go do what I said. I know you think you grown, but grown men live on their own. And as long as you livin' in my house, eatin' my food, you're not gonna be walking around looking like a thug. You see how your brother's dressed? Like somebody with some sense. Now go change!"

Al looked like he wanted to say something, but then

thought better of it and stomped back into his room to change clothes.

"You'll have to excuse my son," Mrs. Taylor explained. "He and C.J. are just total opposites."

C.J. looked a little embarrassed. He'd told Jasmine about how Al had to attend an alternative school because he kept getting kicked out of public school for skipping class. But I could tell he was protective of his little brother. "Mama, you know Al has his own style. But he'll find his own way eventually. And I told you guys to stop comparing us. Al is already acting out because of it."

Mrs. Taylor patted her son's cheek. "My baby, always analyzing people." She turned to Jasmine, ignoring what C.J. had just said. "That's why he can be a psychiatrist or something if he's not a professional athlete."

C.J. sighed like he was used to this conversation with his mother. He looked at me and smiled. "Anyway, thanks for entertaining my girl while I got ready, but we're about to roll out."

My girl! I quickly looked over at Jasmine to see her reaction to that comment. She was cheesin' from ear to ear so hard I wanted to crack up laughing.

"C.J., I wish you wouldn't use that slang with me like I'm your road dog," his mom said.

"My bad . . . I mean, I'm sorry, Mother. We are about to leave," he said sweetly. "And by the way, nobody says 'road dog' anymore."

His mother playfully swatted at him as he darted toward the door.

"And get your car fixed this week," his father called out

after him. "Ain't no son of mine gonna have a girl come pick him up. Taylor men do the picking up."

"Yes, Dad," C.J. called out, grabbing Jasmine's hand and closing the door behind us. "Come on, you guys. Let's get out of here before my folks embarrass me even more."

I eyed Jasmine. I knew exactly what she was thinking—both of their families were crazy, another reason they were a match made in Heaven.

4

Angel

"How many of you think something is wrong with loving yourself?" Miss Rachel slowly walked over to the table where Jasmine was sitting, while she waited for someone to answer.

"Isn't that kind of arrogant?" I asked.

"Unh-unh," Camille said. "Because you need to love yourself before you can expect anyone else to love you, ain't that right, Miss Rachel?"

"It sure is," Rachel said, looking over Jasmine's shoulder. We were at our weekly Good Girlz meeting. Tameka, one of the Good Girlz who joined last year, had moved to Dallas to help out her sick grandmother, so it was just Camille, Alexis, Jasmine, and me. Miss Rachel had asked how we felt about trying to get more girls to join, but we weren't really feeling the idea. We liked having a small, intimate group. We still mentored young girls and did community service projects, so it's not like we never interacted with other people.

"Jasmine, why do you think it's arrogant to love yourself?" Rachel asked.

All eyes were on Jasmine, but she was so busy doodling on her paper that she didn't notice. She finally looked up when she heard us giggling.

"What? Why y'all staring at me?" she said.

Miss Rachel grabbed the paper off the table. "If you weren't over here writing out 'C.J. and Jasmine Taylor' in a heart, maybe you'd know what was going on." She looked closer at the paper. "And who are Cassidy and Calvin the third?"

We laughed harder as Jasmine blushed. Miss Rachel looked clueless.

"Well, who are they?"

"Those are their kids." Camille snickered.

Rachel's eyebrows raised. "Girl, you don't need to be thinking about any kids!"

"That's for sure," I muttered. Miss Rachel knew what she was talking about. She'd been a teenage mom herself—twice. She had her first child at sixteen, then her second at nineteen. She'll be the first to admit she was wild as a teen, but she'd calmed down, learned from her mistakes, and now was dedicated to helping us not make the same mistakes.

"I'm not trying to have any kids now. I was just doodling," Jasmine snapped, reaching up to grab the piece of paper back.

Miss Rachel moved it out of her reach. "Pay attention." She tossed the paper back on the table. "Now, we meet with the girls from Dowling Middle School next week. I want us to talk about self-love and dispel the notion that it's arrogant to love yourself."

We spent a few more minutes discussing our mentoring meeting next week, then we looked up to see Jasmine's brother sticking his head into the room.

"Hello, Jaquan," Rachel said.

"Hey, Miss Rachel," Jaquan replied. He paused when his eyes met Alexis's. They'd briefly dated last year, and even though he'd done her wrong, I think he still kinda liked her. "Hey, Alexis."

Camille wiggled her neck. "Hey, boy. Is Alexis the only person you see?"

Jaquan smiled. "Sorry. What's up, Camille and Angel?" We said hello as he turned his attention to Jasmine. "Hey, Mama said come on. She got called in to work and needs to drop us off."

Jasmine gathered up her things. "I could've just had Alexis or Miss Rachel take me home," she said.

"Well, we're here now. Let's go," he replied.

"Jaquan, I saw the article about you in the *Houston Defender* sports section. I'm so proud of you. Captain of the basketball team and you're only a sophomore?" Miss Rachel said.

Jaquan looked like he was eating up her praise. "Thanks."

"Please don't blow his head up any more than it already is," Jasmine said as she headed toward the door.

"You're just jealous 'cause you can't even dribble a basketball, even though you're ten feet tall," he playfully said.

"Um, excuse me, I can play basketball. I just don't want to. Besides, just because I'm tall doesn't mean I have to play ball. Maybe I'm gonna be a model."

Jaquan was quiet for a moment as he looked at his sister, then he busted out with a loud laugh. It made us all start laughing as well.

Jasmine rolled her eyes as she walked out the door. "Bye, y'all."

"You? A model? Ha ha ha." Jaquan continued cracking up laughing as he followed her out. "Girl, you are so funny."

Their little exchange was cute and had me wishing I had a brother myself. Because, although she would never admit it, there was no denying that Jasmine loved her little brother.

5

Angel

I was tired of being broke. I was tired of struggling, and it was time Marcus helped me out. That's why I found myself standing on Marcus's front porch.

After Marcus dissed me and told me he didn't want anything to do with me or my baby, I had promised myself that I would never ask him for anything. But here I stood contemplating whether or not I should ring the doorbell. I hated even to be here, but raising a baby alone was more than I had bargained for. And my girls were right. It wasn't fair that Marcus got off scot-free with no responsibilities.

I stood there for what seemed like forever before I finally turned to walk home. *Forget this! He's not even worth my giving him the time of day,* I thought.

Angelica was with my sister while she did laundry at our house, and I needed to get back home. Just as I reached the end of the driveway, Marcus pulled up in his beat-up 1999 Hyundai Accent. From the look on his face, I could tell he was not happy to see me.

Marcus threw the car in park and jumped out.

"What are you doing here? I know you didn't have the nerve to just show up at my house," he screamed at me. It had practically taken an act of Congress to get his address. Alexis had slipped somebody in the principal's office fifty dollars to get it from his school file.

Marcus was tall, had caramel-colored skin, and reminded me of the singer Omarian. I used to think he was cute. Not anymore.

I folded my arms with attitude, ready for the fight that was sure to come. "Well, hello to you, too. I came because we need to talk."

Marcus got so close in my face that I could feel his breath on my cheek. Usually, having a guy that close to me would be great, but not Marcus. Just the sight of him now made me sick to my stomach because I hated him so much.

"I told you, we ain't got nothing to talk about," he said.

"But I need help, Marcus. Angelica is both of our responsibilities," I said, thinking maybe if I talked calmly and tried to reason with him, he'd come to his senses.

"I told you not to have the doggone baby in the first place. That was your choice so it's your problem. You deal with it. Besides, I don't even know if that baby is mine. I oughta call the *Maury* show and have him do a paternity test. I can hear Maury now. 'Marcus, when it comes to two-year-old Angelica, you are not the father!' " Marcus said in his best Maury imitation.

At this point my blood was boiling. I couldn't believe this idiot was standing here denying my baby and calling me a tramp in the process. He knows he was my first, yet he insisted on acting like a jerk. I could feel the tears forming in my eyes. I had to calm myself down before I spoke.

"I can't believe you. And my baby is eighteen months old, not two years. But I guess you wouldn't know that since you've never laid eyes on her since she was born."

Marcus laughed. "Personally, I don't care if I ever see you or her again in my life. Like I told you before, I don't want any kids right now. I have the rest of my life to think about. I can't go to college with a kid on my back."

I looked at Marcus and shook my head. What in the world did I ever see in that boy? I can't believe I was even attracted to him in the first place. When we first met he was so sweet and always saying just the right thing to make me smile from ear to ear. I just knew he was "the one." Now when I looked at him, I hated his guts. I was definitely going to have to talk to Miss Rachel and ask her how I can learn not to hate someone.

Just then the front door opened. A sickly looking woman wearing a tattered peach housecoat stuck her head out.

"Marcus, is that you? What's going on out here?" The woman looked like she had once been very pretty, but now her eyes looked like they were sinking into her head and her skin looked ashy. Her stringy black hair was pulled back in a bun.

"Yeah, Ma. It's nothing." He stepped in front of me. "Just let me handle this and I'll be on inside."

I couldn't believe that was his mother. She looked so different. I'd met her one time—when my mom and I went to their old house to tell her about the baby. But she'd believed Marcus when he said the baby wasn't his, so she'd been no help. My mom was so disgusted that we hadn't contacted her again.

His mom strained her head, trying to get a better look at me. "Is that—?"

"Ma, please, go lie down. I'll be in in a minute. You shouldn't be up anyway."

She sighed as if she didn't really feel like arguing. "Okay, baby. Did you get my medicine?"

Marcus held up a small brown bag that I hadn't even noticed in his hand. "I got it. Now go on and I'll be in to give it to you in a minute."

She nodded, slowly closing the door.

"Look, you decided to have that baby, so she's your problem."

"You know what, Marcus?" I said, quickly forgetting about his mother. "Whether or not you wanted a kid, you got one. If you didn't want a baby, then you shouldn't have been doing anything that makes babies. Neither of us should have. But she's here now and she has needs. My daughter needs a father in her life. If you can't do that, the least you can do is make sure she's taken care of." I paused before continuing. "I just thought I would let you know that my mom and I are thinking about taking you to court for child support." I hadn't talked to my mother about that at all. But it had just come to me, and I was thinking that might spur him to do the right thing.

"What!" Marcus screamed. "You know doggone well I ain't got no money."

"Whatever, Marcus. I just need help."

"Look, I'm done talking to you. Get away from my house," Marcus said as he walked up the front walk.

"How are you going to feel when your little girl is calling some other man daddy?" I yelled. Now, that was funny. I hadn't been out on a date since Marcus. So I had no prospects at all. But at this point, I was trying anything to get Marcus's attention.

Marcus stopped, turned, and looked at me. For a split second it looked like what I'd said had gotten through to him. But then he shook his head, walked inside, and slammed the door.

6

Jasmine

"You so stupid you have to put lipstick on your head just to make up your mind."

I looked over at my brother and laughed. "You so stupid you tried to put M&M's in alphabetical order."

"You so fat I tried to drive around you and ran out of gas," he said.

"You so corny you should be in a field."

He looked at me, paused, then busted out laughing. "Okay, now, *that* was corny."

"It was, wasn't it?" I admitted. I guess I'd been hanging around Alexis too long because she was known for her corny comments.

I actually couldn't believe how much fun Jaquan and

I were having just walking and talking. My grandmother had sent me to the corner store to get some cooking oil so she could finish frying chicken for dinner. (It seemed like we were always having chicken for dinner.) Out of the blue, Jaquan had offered to walk with me, which definitely caught me off guard because my brother didn't *offer* to do anything. When I tried to ask him what was up, he made like he wanted to buy himself some candy from the store. But I had seen two bags of Skittles in his backpack earlier. Even so, I let it slide. I just figured we were finally getting to the point where we enjoyed each other's company.

"So, what did the coach say about you being on the McDonald's All-American team?" I asked. I was so proud of Jaquan. Only three boys in the whole city of Houston had made it onto the national McDonald's All-American basketball team, and my brother was one of them. He was blowing people away with his skills on the basketball court. And he knew he was good, but that didn't stop him from getting out there and practicing every single day, and I think it was definitely making him even better.

"Coach said I'm gonna have Division One colleges beating down my door."

My eyes widened. This was the first time my brother had ever mentioned college, at least with so much enthusiasm.

"I know I have two more years, but I'm tellin' you, if I have a shot at getting out of this dump"—he motioned around at the neighborhood—"then I'm takin' it. Plus, get this, Coach even said I shouldn't be surprised if the pro scouts start looking at me."

I stopped and turned to him. "What?"

"I know, I know. Every basketball player in the neighborhood thinks they can go pro but I'm not bankin' on that. Yeah, I'd love to, and yeah, I think I'm good enough to make it, but honestly, I'm just trying to get a college degree so I can get a good job, then get us all out of this neighborhood. It's gettin' rougher by the day. By the time Jahcim and Jalen get to high school, it's gon' be nothin' but trouble on every corner. The streets are rough."

His suddenly serious tone caught me off guard. Now that I thought about it, lately he had more and more moments like this, when he would all of a sudden turn serious. Maybe it was all just part of him growing up.

We made our way inside the store and I picked up the cooking grease and a loaf of bread. I smiled inside as I noted that Jaquan didn't buy any candy. He just stood around as I paid for my stuff. We exited the store and I was just about to call him on it when four boys in baggy pants passed by us. They were cursing, laughing, and talking loudly.

The expression on Jaquan's face tensed up when he spotted them.

"Well, if it isn't Jaquan Jones," the short, stocky one in the front said. All four boys stopped in front of us on the sidewalk.

"What's up?" Jaquan said unenthusiastically.

"Same ol', same ol'." The guy stroked his chin. "I thought I told you to get wit' me."

"I've been a little busy," Jaquan replied. His whole body looked tense. "I'm just tryin' to stay focused on playing ball."

The guy threw up his hands. "Hey, I'm not a difficult brotha. I can respect that. But I also think you can show us a little love, too."

"You don't need my love, Tonio. Looks like you got plenty of it," Jaquan said, motioning to the boys behind him.

These guys were freaking me out. Two of them wore hoodies, and they all looked shady and like they'd just been dropped off by the prison truck. When I noticed two teardrops on Tonio's face, I knew that wasn't a good sign.

"Yo, man. I'm gonna be looking to hear from you," Tonio said.

"Yeah, whatever," Jaquan replied.

"Hey, foxy mama," Tonio said, turning his attention to me. He licked his lips as he looked me up and down like I was a pork chop sandwich.

"Umm, is this 1975? *Foxy mama*? Are you for real?" I asked.

He got in my face. He barely came to my chin. "Get with me and I'll show you how real I am."

I took two steps backward. "Get out of my face before I show you how real *I* am."

Jaquan rested his hand on my lower arm. "Jasmine, chill."

Tonio broke out in a huge grin. "See, that's what I'm talkin' 'bout. A tough girl. You don't seem like you're scurred of nothin'."

"Am I supposed to be *scurred* of you?"

Tonio laughed. "Shoot, while I'm talking to Jaquan, I might need to be hollerin' at you. Why don't *you* come see me? The Blood Brothers can always use a good sister."

Jaquan pulled my arm. "Jasmine, let's go," he demanded.

Tonio laughed again. "I'll see you around, pretty lady. Let's bounce," he told his boys.

"*A gang?* You fooling around with a gang?" I asked as we started heading back home.

"Ugggh!" Jaquan groaned, smashing his fist into the palm of his other hand. "Man, I can't believe those dudes."

I shook my head, not believing my brother was messing with a gang. "You don't need to be getting caught up with them, Jaquan."

"I'm not trying to get caught up with them," he said. Little lines were forming in his forehead, which meant he was getting really mad. "That's the problem."

"So they want you to join their gang?"

He waved me off like he was disgusted, and didn't answer.

"Jaquan," I said, pulling his arm to get him to stop walking. "I know you're not even thinking about getting involved with a gang. 'Cuz if they don't kill you, Mama will."

"Man, I ain't with no gang," he said, obviously frustrated. "Didn't you just hear me say I'm tryin' to go to college? I'm tryin' to get out of this neighborhood."

"Okay, I was just checkin'."

"Just drop it." We started walking again.

"Unh-unh," I said. "I'm gonna tell Mama."

"You gonna tell her what? Just keep your big fat mouth shut." He poked his lips out and stomped down the sidewalk. "You make me sick."

I turned up my nose. There was the Jaquan I knew and couldn't stand. But the more I studied him as we walked, the more something didn't seem right. Something in his eyes was different. There was a scared look behind his anger. And that scared me.

I stepped in front of him on the sidewalk, forcing him to stop.

"What are you doing? Move," he said, pushing me aside. Over the past year, my brother had gotten bigger than me, but I was still able to hold my own against him.

"No. Not until you tell me what's goin' on." I placed my hands on my hips to let him know I was serious.

He sighed heavily before saying, "Look, they just got beef with me, that's all. And I don't want any beef. I just want to handle my business and get out of here. And they're makin' it harder and harder to do that. But I need you to just let me handle this, a'ight? Tonio is a lot of talk, that's all. But stay out of it and please don't bring Mama into it."

I didn't know what to say at first, but finally I nodded before stepping aside. We continued walking home in silence, the fear I felt inside getting worse.

7

Jasmine

$\mathcal{I}$ leaned up against the doorway to our apartment to catch my breath. Jaquan hadn't said anything else on the way home and had all but sprinted back. I could tell he was mad, but knowing my brother, I'd just have to let him calm down on his own.

He stomped into the house past Nikki, who was lying on the sofa watching *Flava of Love 3*, probably trying to figure out how she could get on the show.

"What's his problem?" Nikki asked. She looked like one of those hoochies on the show in black lace leggings and a tank top.

I debated telling her what had just happened, but I knew she'd run straight to Mama, so I didn't say anything about it. "Nothing," I replied, closing the front door. "He's just in a foul mood."

"Well, he needs to go somewhere else with that because ain't nobody got time for no attitude."

I narrowed my eyes at her. The attitude queen had the nerve to talk about somebody else's attitude.

"A person can't even watch TV in peace around here," she continued. "That's why I'll be glad when I get my own place," she mumbled.

I wanted to tell her she wouldn't be half as glad as we would, seeing as how she was almost twenty years old. But I just let it slide because it's not like it would've made a difference anyway.

"Where's Granny?" I asked.

"In her skin," Nikki casually replied.

I rolled my eyes at my sister and made my way into the kitchen. My grandmother had left a note on the counter. I read the note out loud. " 'Jasmine, wash the chicken and season it. I had to run next door to Miss Mattie's.' "

I tossed the note back on the counter. Nikki's triflin' behind was sitting right in there on the sofa. Why couldn't she wash and season the chicken?

I had just placed the nasty raw chicken parts on a plate and set it on the counter when the telephone rang. I heard Nikki scream, "I got it!"

Two seconds later she appeared in the kitchen door-way. "Telephone. It's your nerdy friends." She tossed the cordless phone at me. I barely was able to catch it.

"Hello," I said.

"Hey, it's Camille and Alexis," Camille said. "What's wrong with your sister? She was so rude."

"So what else is new?" I said. "My sister is always rude."

Just then Jalen and Jaheim came running through the kitchen, knocking over the plate with the meat. The chicken splattered all over the floor and the plate broke in several pieces. "Gimme back my car!" Jalen wailed as he chased after Jaheim. Neither of them stopped as they ran through the house.

"Ugggh, I hate my life," I said, reaching down to pick up the dirty chicken and broken plate pieces.

"Would you rather go back and stay with your father?" Alexis slyly said.

"Okay, you have a point," I said, thinking about the nightmare of staying with my father last year. He lived in La Marque, which is about forty-five minutes south of Houston. He was big-time in the school district down there, but he was married to the wicked witch of the south. She hated my guts and didn't hesitate to let it be known. After I got in a little trouble, she told my father I had to go. Between that and a whole bunch of secrets about my dad I'd discovered while I was living with them, I'd been all too happy to come back home.

"Anyway," Camille said. "Guess who we saw at the mall?"

"Who?"

"Marcus," Alexis replied.

"Angel's Marcus?"

"Yep, buying the new Jordans. Two pairs," Camille said, the disgust evident in her voice.

"And I saw the price. They were each at least a hundred and fifty bucks," Alexis added.

"What?" I exclaimed.

"Ummm-hmm," Alexis said and tsked. "But he can't buy any diapers for his daughter?"

"That's jacked up, and I was on my way over there to give him a piece of my mind," Camille said. She paused. "But I saw this cute boy come in the store and I got a little distracted." She laughed.

"You are too much," I replied, dumping the broken plate in the trash and putting the chicken in the sink. I'd wash it off and nobody ever had to know it fell on the floor. "Well, did you guys tell Angel yet?"

"We figured we'd all tell her at the meeting," Camille said. "It was just yesterday when she was telling me how hard of a time she was having. They cut back her mom's hours at the library. She wants to get an after-school job, but she has to pick up Angelica from the sitter by six. So she doesn't know what she's going to do."

"Dang, that's messed up. She should make Marcus pay child support," I said.

"I know. I'm gonna tell her that, too," Camille said. "Don't you think we should tell her that, Alexis?"

Alexis didn't answer.

"Hello, Alexis. Are you there? What do you think?"

"I'm here. I'm trying to figure out if I should wear my hair up or down to the party Saturday," Alexis said.

"Ummm, hello. Can you focus, please?" Camille snapped.

"Sorry, all this talk about baby daddies and child support is just too much," Alexis said. "It makes my head hurt."

"Well, how do you think Angel feels?"

"You're right," Alexis said. "Dang, I feel sorry for her."

"Well, you know Angel doesn't want our sympathy. She knows she messed up and she's dealing with it. But she shouldn't have to deal with it by herself."

"You're right about that, Camille," I said.

"So, I say we tell her at the meeting."

"I agree. But look, I need to go before my granny comes in here trippin'," I said.

"Okay, we'll see you tomorrow."

We said our good-byes. I looked at the chicken and decided it could wait another minute. I wanted to check on my brother.

I walked down the hallway, poking my head inside once I got to his room. Jaquan was lying across his bed, lost in thought.

"You okay?" I asked.

"Yeah," he muttered.

I stood there awkwardly for a moment, not really knowing what to say. So I finally walked over, sat down next to him on the bed, and said, "Everything is gonna be fine. You're gonna go to college, then the NBA, and you're going to buy me the flyest Lexus on the market."

"I hope so, Jaz," he said, looking like he was fighting back tears.

"I know so," I replied. Then I did something I don't think I'd ever done before. I leaned in and softly kissed my brother on the head. "I love you, Jaquan."

"I love you, too, big sis." He paused. "Don't you have that Good Girlz meeting tomorrow?"

"Yeah."

"Y'all be prayin' there?"

"Yeah," I said, wondering where he was going with this.

"Can you . . . can you, um, say a prayer for me? You know, that I work all this out."

I felt tears forming in my eyes. It hurt to see my brother with so much weighing on him.

"You know what?" I said, surprising myself again. "How 'bout I don't wait until tomorrow night and we both pray right now?"

I didn't give him a chance to respond as I took his hand, kneeled, pulled him down next to me, and said a prayer for God to keep my brother safe.

8

Angel

"Would you calm down already?" I hissed to Jasmine. She was standing there with her lips poked out, tapping her foot like she was really irritated with me or something.

"I'm ready to go," she said.

"Just chill. We're just hanging out," I replied. Today was the first sunny day this year, so the basketball court at Jasmine's apartment complex was packed. More than thirty guys were out playing, and just as many girls were out watching.

"What part of 'I don't want to hang out with my brother and his buster friends' do you not get?" she said. "You were supposed to be coming over here so we can work on our biology project. Not so we can come out here and watch these fools on the basketball court thinking they LeBron James."

"But they're so cute."

She turned up her nose. "Who? Who's cute?"

I pointed to a light-skinned guy with green eyes. "Pretty Ricky for one." Jasmine rolled her eyes as I continued. "That boy right there for two," I said, pointing at another tall, cute guy who was dribbling the ball.

"Junior? Ewww."

"And your brother for three," I continued. "Look at him with his shirt off. Whew, Lord." I fanned myself with my hand.

"Ugggh. I think I just threw up," she said, making a gagging noise.

I pushed her shoulder. "Girl, you know your brother is fine."

"Whatever, Angel. Haven't we already learned our lesson with Alexis trying to talk to him?"

It was my turn to roll my eyes. That had been a disaster. Alexis had briefly dated Jaquan, against Jasmine's advice, and when he'd dumped her, Alexis and Jasmine fell out. Luckily, we don't stay mad at one another for long.

"I ain't trying to talk to Jaquan," I finally said. "I just said he's fine. I like being out here looking at all these boys on the basketball court. Look, isn't that Al, C.J.'s brother?"

I hadn't even noticed Al out on the court. I looked up just as he tried to slam-dunk the basketball but missed and toppled to the ground. Everybody on the court busted out laughing.

"Dog, you think you a superstar athlete like your brother or something?" Junior taunted as he stood over Al. "Go play over there." He pointed to a group of small kids who looked like they were eight or nine, playing kickball in the field across from the basketball court. "That's more your speed." That brought even more laughter. Al clenched his jaw as he pulled himself up off the ground.

Junior grabbed the basketball, turned, and took off toward the hoop, making a clean slam dunk that sent the crowd into a frenzy. He looked over at me to make sure I was watching and I gave him a huge smile.

"He ain't doing nothin' but showboating," Jasmine said.

I giggled.

"Look, I'm out," Jasmine said, exasperated. "My mama and grandma are gone. I'm going to watch BET videos."

"I'll be up there in a minute," I called out as she walked off.

I sat taking in the game for a few more minutes. I didn't like basketball really. But I liked cute guys. And there were plenty of them out today.

"You see that?" Junior yelled as he dunked on someone. "You see that, pretty little *mami*?" he said again before I realized he was talking to me.

I smiled and nodded. I was surprised. Usually I was the shy one, but I seemed to be coming out of my shell since I'd been in the Good Girlz.

Junior and his friends stopped their game when another group of five boys walked up to them. Three of the boys wore black jackets with hoods. All of their jeans looked like they were about to fall off. I started to get an uneasy feeling in my stomach. But when the leader of the new group smiled, it seemed like everything was going to be all right.

"What's up?" the leader asked as he approached Junior and his friends.

"It's you, Tonio," Junior replied, giving him some dap. Tonio looked like he was about nineteen years old. He had braids zigzagging across his head. Two gold teeth shined in his mouth and tattoos covered his arm.

Jaquan, who was holding the basketball, shot the new boys a disgusted look, then told his friends, "Yo, I'm out." He reached down and picked up his T-shirt before heading off.

"Awww, J, don't leave on our account," Tonio said, throwing up his hands.

Jaquan held up his hands in surrender. "Look, Tonio, I don't want no trouble. My leavin' ain't got nothin' to do with you."

"But the game wasn't over," Tonio protested. The whole court had gotten quiet as everyone watched the scene unfold. A lot of people looked nervous, including Junior and his friends. Al seemed to be the only one who didn't look scared. In fact, he was staring at Tonio in awe.

"I'm good," Jaquan said.

"You know, I think I'm offended," Tonio said, walking closer to Jaquan. "Whenever I come around, you jet. Whenever I stop and talk to you, you ain't got no words for me. What? You think you're too good for a brother? You too good to hang out with the Blood Brothers?"

"Looks to me like you got more than enough people to hang out with," Jaquan said, eyeing the guys behind Tonio.

"But we can always use one more, especially one who might make a name for himself. Boy, you got game on that court." Tonio nodded knowingly.

Jaquan slipped his T-shirt over his head. "I know. And for the hundredth time, I'm not interested in your little gang." Jaquan looked like he regretted the words as soon as they slipped out.

The smile left Tonio's face. He turned around and looked at his boys. "Did you hear that? He's not interested in our *little* gang."

Several of the boys frowned up, and I could tell trouble was about to break out.

"Boy, you'd betta recognize this *little* gang," Tonio spat, stepping toward Jaquan.

My heart stopped as I watched Jaquan, who didn't back down. Jaquan's friends hadn't said a word. Junior looked scared to death, and Pretty Ricky was hiding behind some trash cans.

"Tonio, man, just chill," Jaquan calmly said. "I don't want drama. I told you that ain't where I'm at. I have respect for you and your crew, but that just ain't me. I'm out." With that, Jaquan turned and walked off the court.

Tonio hesitated, then reached down and picked up the basketball Jaquan had dropped. He threw it as hard as he could, hitting Jaquan in the back of the head. Jaquan stumbled.

"Did I say I was through talkin' to you?" Tonio yelled.

Jaquan rubbed his head as he slowly turned around.

No, no, no, I silently wielded. This guy looked like he wasn't one to be played with. *Just walk away, Jaquan.*

"You don't leave until I tell you to leave," Tonio announced. "You don't disrespect me like that, fool."

Jaquan looked like he was thinking, and common sense must've prevailed because he chuckled, shook his head, then turned back around and kept walking.

I could tell Tonio didn't like being dissed in front of everybody. His boys were looking at him like they couldn't believe he was going to let Jaquan just go like that. Tonio nodded his head like he was trying to calm himself down.

"Big mistake, brotha. Big mistake," he mumbled before turning and walking off the court himself.

9

Jasmine

"Are you sure you're gonna be okay? You've been in a funk all day." Alexis's high-pitched voice snapped me out of my thoughts. We had just wrapped up the Good Girlz meeting and were standing outside as I waited on C.J. to pick me up.

"Yeah, Jasmine," Rachel said as she walked out to join us. "Your body was at tonight's meeting, but your mind was somewhere else." She leaned in and whispered in my ear. "We can go back inside if you need to talk," she said.

I sighed heavily as I looked back and forth between my girls and Miss Rachel. Everybody looked genuinely concerned. I *had* been out of it. I was still thinking about what Angel had told me yesterday about what happened on the basketball court. Then, to top things off, my brother was in a true funk, something he'd been in a lot lately. And I wasn't used to that. As annoying as Jaquan was, he still was always the happy-go-lucky type. So for him to walk around mad at the world like he'd been doing the last few weeks meant that this was more serious than I'd originally thought. I'd tried to talk to him about it, but of course he blew me off. Now, based on what Angel said went down at the basketball court and our little run-in on the way to the convenience store, I knew Jaquan might be in over his head.

"Naw, I'm straight," I finally said, turning my attention back to my friends. "Just got a lot on my mind."

"Well, you know I'm here for you if you want to talk," Rachel said, her voice laced with concern.

"And I'm here, too, boo." We all turned to the little boy standing behind Rachel. He had deep dimples and his hazel eyes were shining brightly as he cheesed and licked his lips. He was so cute and might have had girls falling all over him—if he wasn't ten years old.

"Jordan Kobe Clark, if you don't get your little manish behind in that church . . ." Rachel chastised.

We all laughed.

"Aww, Ma, why you gotta make me look bad in front of the ladies?" he whined. "You gon' mess up my game."

"Boy, you ain't got no game," she said, swatting at his behind. "Get inside."

He flashed a smile as he looked at Jasmine. "Call me, baby," he said, putting his thumb and little finger to his ear and mouth, mimicking a phone. "I'll help you forget all your troubles." Then he darted inside as his mother swatted at him again.

"Forgive my little grown son," Rachel said. "I think he's been sneaking and watching BET or something because he's losing his ever-lovin' mind." She shook her head as she followed him inside.

"That boy is too funny," Alexis said, checking her makeup in the mirror of her compact.

"He's gonna be a little heartbreaker with his cute self," Camille added.

I smiled—Jordan and Rachel's little episode had actually made me smile. "He is cute, but he's bad as all get-out," I added.

"On the real, Jasmine, are you sure you're okay?" Camille asked. "I mean, I know you're worried about your brother, but it's gonna be okay."

"I know," I replied, my mood souring again. I could tell Angel, Alexis, and Camille were just as worried as me, and their trying to make me feel better meant a lot, especially since Angel was dealing with her own drama with Marcus. Camille and Alexis had told her about seeing Marcus at the mall. Angel had called him but he wouldn't return her calls.

"Well, I see something that will definitely put you in a good mood," Camille sang as she eyed the white Grand Am pulling into the church parking lot.

As soon as he pulled onto the church grounds, C.J. respectfully turned off his music. I broke out in a huge grin as I watched him come to a stop in front of me.

"Hey, pretty lady. Want a ride?" he said, leaning out the window.

"My mama told me not to get in the car with strangers," I joked.

"It's okay. Your mama said I'm cool since I'm gonna be your future husband and all."

"Awwww," Camille, Angel, and Alexis said at the same time.

"What's up, ladies?" C.J. said.

"Nothing," Camille replied. "What's up with you?"

"Hey, C.J.," Alexis and Angel said in unison.

"Well, see you guys later," I said, still grinning. I walked over to the passenger side of the car.

"She is so lucky," I heard Camille mumble as I got in the car. I felt lucky. C.J.'s contagious smile always made me feel better.

We made small talk on the drive home, but I guess my melancholy mood crept back up on me because it wasn't long before C.J. could tell something was wrong.

"Jasmine, are you gonna talk to me?" he asked as he pulled up behind my apartment complex. I had him drop me off in the back because I didn't want my mom or my granny tripping about his giving me a ride home this late.

"I can tell something is wrong," he added when I didn't reply.

I exhaled. "You're right. I have a lot on my mind." I told him my fears about Jaquan's getting caught up in a gang.

C.J. surprised me when he said, "I know exactly what

you're feeling. My brother, Al, is going through the exact same thing. The only problem is he's feelin' the idea, which is totally crazy to me."

My mouth dropped open. "What? You mean Al is getting caught up in a gang?"

C.J. looked momentarily distressed. "Yeah. It's the new group of boys he's been hanging around with. Ever since his best friend moved away, he's been running with the wrong crowd. They're the ones had him skipping school in the first place. Now Al is always talking about how those dudes in the gang are cool and how they make everyone respect them. For some reason he's gotten this thing with wanting people to respect him. I think he believes he'll get respect if he hooks up with a gang. Man, my mom and dad would go ballistic if they found out."

"Well, Jaquan is trying to go to college and he doesn't want to get wrapped up with a gang at all, but I can tell something's going on that he's not telling me," I said.

C.J. softly squeezed my hand. "Don't worry, Jasmine. It'll all work out. I'll say a prayer for both of our brothers."

I reached over and hugged him, feeling much better and saying a prayer myself, thanking God for sending me such a wonderful boyfriend.

10

Angel

I loved my daughter, Angelica, to death, but I wasn't gonna lie, being a single teenage mom was hard.

It's funny, you always hear people talking about how you can get pregnant your first time. But most people my age don't believe that. Well, I'm living proof. That's what happened to me. I let Marcus convince me that "if I loved him, I'd get with him." I finally—against my better judgment—gave in. And as soon as I found out I was pregnant, I found out it was Marcus who didn't really love *me*. He said he had no intention of being a father. It's messed up how boys can just up and say that, but me, I didn't have a choice. That's why what Miss Rachel says about it being up to the girls to protect themselves is so true. Marcus jetted and left me to take care of my baby by myself. I had threatened him with suing for child support, but who was I kidding? He didn't and wouldn't work, not if it meant he had to give me one dime.

Having a baby was so hard. My mom wasn't playing when she said I was gonna have to take responsibility. It could get pretty depressing sometimes. Shoot, my girls were at a basketball game right now, but I couldn't go because I didn't have a babysitter and my mom was at her second job at the bakery. Between getting left out of stuff and the way Marcus acts, my life wasn't no joke. Making matters worse was the fact that I didn't even have a car, so it wasn't like I could even really go anywhere most of the time.

The only reason I was out now was because my sister had to drop in for a quick meeting at her job. I rode along to take Angelica to the park next door to the building where Rosario worked as a receptionist for an insurance agency.

I watched as Angelica took a scoop of dirt in the sand-box and poured it all over her head.

"Look, Mommy," she sang, laughing as the sand poured down her face.

I jumped up and raced over to try and clean her up. "Angelica, look at you," I said, picking her up.

Sand was all in her hair. When some of it fell into her eyes, she began crying.

"Mommy, it hurts," she cried.

I rushed to the bathroom to get her washed up. She squirmed and whined as I tried to get the sand out of her face and hair.

"Finally," I mumbled when I was satisfied that she was clean, and I took her hand to lead her out. I stopped when I saw Al, C.J.'s brother, pull another boy behind the side of the park restroom.

Normally, I don't eavesdrop on people, but the distressed look on his face had piqued my interest.

"Here," I said, pulling a sucker out of my bag and handing it to Angelica to keep her quiet. She tore the paper off and happily began sucking it as I backed up and leaned against the wall and listened to their conversation.

"Man, what am I going to do?" Al said.

I didn't know who he was talking to, but the guy responded, "I don't know either, man. It ain't like you got much choice though. I told you about foolin' with Tonio 'n'em. Dang, man. Your folks are gon' kill you if they find out you in a gang."

"Look, don't start preachin' to me," Al huffed.

"I'm just sayin'. You're in trouble."

"Tell me about it." I heard him sigh heavily. "They want me to shoot him, talking 'bout nobody can disrespect a Blood Brother and live to talk about it. I can't believe they want me to kill him."

"That's what gangs do. I think you should go to the police."

"Are you crazy? Then *I'll* be the one getting shot."

"I told you not to mess with them."

"Raymond, look—"

"Okay, okay, my bad. I just don't take you for a killer."

"I'm not."

"Well, why you wanna be in a gang anyway? I mean, look at C.J. He's about to go to college and he's got a good chance of playing pro."

"Raymond, I'm not my brother, the superstar athlete who brings home good grades and never gets in any trouble. And I don't wanna be him. I'm sick and tired of everybody always trying to make me out to be like him. I'm just me, and when I'm hanging out with Tonio 'n'em, I ain't got to worry 'bout nobody trippin' 'cause I'm such a failure, like my moms never hesitates to tell me."

"Whatever, man. I heard your mom trip before and she ain't talking about you being a failure. She just trips because you're always in some kind of trouble," Raymond said.

"Whatever, just keep your mouth shut, okay?"

"You're my best friend. You know I ain't gonna say nothin'. But I don't know how you gonna get out of this one. And ain't your brother dating his sister?"

My eyes grew wide.

"Yeah, man. That chick got C.J.'s nose so wide open. That's why this is so jacked up. But Tonio is serious. He said Jaquan can't get away with dissin' him in front of everybody." He paused. "Maybe I can just shoot at him and miss."

"What kind of gangsta are you?" Raymond laughed.

"One that ain't trying to go to jail."

"Mommy, I hun-gy," Angelica said, snapping my attention away from their conversation. I picked her up, covered her mouth, and raced back in the girls' restroom. I don't know if Al and Raymond overheard Angelica, but just in case, I hid in a bathroom stall, fighting Angelica, who was trying to get down, for at least fifteen minutes. If Al was contemplating shooting someone, then there's no telling what he could do to me.

Finally, I eased to the door. I needed to go find Jasmine. I poked my head out to make sure the coast was clear. Then I scooped up my daughter and raced out of the park.

I made my way next door to my sister's office.

"Well, hello, Angel," one of her co-workers said. "And look at this precious one." She leaned in and tousled Angelica's hair.

"Hi, Mrs. Barbara. May I use the telephone?"

"Only if you let me take this little one back to the break room. I have some apple slices with your name on them." She squeezed Angelica's cheek.

"App'es," Angelica said, clasping her hands together, before reaching up to go with Mrs. Barbara.

I sat down at Rosario's desk and immediately picked up the phone and punched in Camille's cell phone number. It went straight to voice mail. I didn't leave a message, but instead I quickly hung up and dialed Alexis's number. The phone rang four times, then went to the voice mail also. They probably were having such a blast that they couldn't hear their phones.

"Mommy, app'es," Angelica said, racing over to me and holding up an apple slice. I nodding distractedly as I tried to figure out my next move. Angelica nibbled on her apple slice for a few minutes before spotting the candy bowl on Rosario's desk. "Can-dy, Mommy, can-dy," she said.

I reached in, grabbed a peppermint, handed it to her, then waved her away as it dawned on me to call Jasmine's house and just warn Jaquan myself. I punched in the number, but their phone was disconnected, something Jasmine said usually happened around the same time every month.

"Rosario is just gonna have to take me over there," I mumbled. I was about to go check how much longer my sister would be in her meeting when I heard Mrs. Barbara scream.

"Oh, my!" she said, racing over to Angelica, who was sitting on the floor gagging.

My eyes widened in horror as I watched my baby's olive complexion turn blue.

"She's choking! She's choking!" Mrs. Barbara yelled.

I glanced at the empty peppermint wrapper on the floor and my heart dropped. I immediately grabbed her and started pounding her back. "Spit it out!" I screamed.

Her little body started convulsing, and Mrs. Barbara yelled, "Don't hit her. You'll make it worse! Give her here!"

I ignored her and continued shaking my baby. "Angelica, spit it out!" I cried.

"She can't spit it out! She's choking!"

The next thing I knew, another of Rosario's co-workers had grabbed Angelica from me and wrapped her arms around my daughter's chest. "One, two, three." She panted, squeezing Angelica's chest. "One, two, three." She squeezed again.

By this point, everyone in the office had raced out into

the reception area, and I was in tears. I was just about to snatch my baby back when the small red and white piece of candy came flying out of her mouth. Angelica gagged, coughed, then let out a wail.

Rosario reached out and took her, trying to comfort her. I was too stunned to move and could only slump to the floor in tears.

ll

Jasmine

I so could not believe I was acting all giddy and stuff. I was blushing and giggling. You gotta understand, I don't blush and I dang sure don't giggle. But for some reason that's how I got whenever I was around C.J. He was different from my last boyfriend, Donovan. Donovan was cool and all, but he had an image to uphold, so he was always acting cool. He let me know he was feeling me, but not like C.J. did. And C.J. didn't care what anyone said. If he wanted to shout his feelings from the rooftop, he was going to do just that.

"So, I was thinking, if I get a football scholarship at Grambling, like I'm hoping for, you could come, too," he said. We were returning from getting something to eat and were slowly making our way up the walkway to my apartment complex. I didn't want the night to end, especially now that C.J. was making plans for our future.

"Grambling?" I said.

"Yeah," he said excitedly as he stopped and turned toward me. "I'd have to stay in the football dorm, but I'm sure it would be close to your dorm and we could see each other whenever we wanted. Shoot, you could even spend the night if you wanted."

My eyes lit up. My being able to do what I wanted? Come and go as I pleased? And even spend the night with my man? Oh, college was going to be all that. I was just about to share my thoughts with C.J. when we noticed the commotion. People were running like crazy from the basketball court. Some people were screaming, others were crying.

"What in the world?" I mumbled. I saw one of my neighbors racing past me. I grabbed her arm. "Shayla, what's going on?"

Her eyes widened in horror when she saw me. "Oh, my God. Jasmine . . ."

"What?" Shayla was the true definition of a project chick, so to see her about to cry had my heart racing.

"A-are you just getting here?" she said, looking back and forth between me and C.J.

I nodded. "Yeah, what's up?"

She glanced back toward the basketball court. "Your brother . . . Blood . . . it just all happened so fast."

I shook her. "Shayla, what are you talking about?"

"Jaquan!" she cried. She used to have a crush on him

in middle school, so what happened must've been bad for her to be all shaken up like that.

"What about Jaquan?" I asked. It was obvious Shayla wasn't going to provide me with any answers. She was in full-fledged crying mode now.

I looked around. People had stopped running and they were all standing around pointing toward the basketball court, C.J. right behind me. I heard words like "gun," "shots," and "that poor boy."

I took off running toward the basketball court. I had a sick feeling in my gut and began yelling for my brother. "Jaquan! Jaquan!"

I stopped dead in my tracks as I reached the entrance to the basketball court. I recognized the bright yellow sweatpants immediately. There was a pool of blood underneath them. My heart dropped and everything seemed to go in slow motion as my eyes made their way up my brother's lifeless body.

The only thing I remembered after that was letting out a heart-wrenching scream and collapsing into C.J.'s arms.

12

Jasmine

I still couldn't believe my brother was gone. It had been only a couple of days since we buried him and I was still waiting for him to walk into my room and say, "What's up, big head?" I smiled through the tears running down my cheeks as I thought of how much our relationship had evolved over the past year.

"God, why did You take my brother?" I cried. I was lying across my bed looking up at the ceiling and wondering why God would do this to our family, when my grandmother came into my room.

"Jasmine, don't you be in here questioning God. He knew what He was doin'."

I turned over onto my back. I was so not in the mood for one of her sermons about how good God is.

"I know you're angry right now, but you have to remember that everything happens for a reason and this was all in God's plan," she continued, walking over to me. My grandmother was superreligious, no matter how bad things got or how hard of a time we had. But while I had grown spiritually, I just didn't have her faith.

"What kind of God kills kids?" I said before I realized the words had actually come out of my mouth.

My grandmother pursed her lips. "Now, don't get slapped in the mouth up in here." She took a deep breath like she was trying not to get upset herself. "God doesn't kill kids. That's all the work of the devil. We just have to remain faithful that everything that happens is in His order—even if we don't understand it."

For the life of me, I couldn't understand the reasoning behind that line of thinking. I mean, I knew I shouldn't be questioning God, but I couldn't see what His reason was for taking my brother.

I studied my grandmother. I knew she'd loved Jaquan to death, yet she was so strong. Old folks had so much insight. I guess that once you get old, you've seen so much death that it just doesn't affect you the way it does everyone else.

My grandmother was still preaching to me, but at that point I had tuned her out, until I heard her mention C.J.'s name. She had just finished saying that he was at the front door wanting to see me.

"Grandma, why didn't you tell me he was here in the first place? I look a mess," I said, dabbing my eyes.

"I see you ain't too sad," she said lightheartedly. "You sho' perked up at the mention of that little boy's name."

I sighed. There had been so many people around after the funeral that I hadn't really had a chance to talk to C.J. "Granny, can you tell him I'll be out in a second?"

My grandmother walked out the room mumbling about how she wasn't "no doggone secretary." I was actually happy that C.J. had taken the time to come and see about me. He and my friends had been great since Jaquan was shot. They had all been calling to check on me, and I had even managed to hold conversations with them a couple of times. Angel was acting all strange, but I just figured she didn't know how to deal with the situation. I mean, I was having a hard time dealing with it myself. Camille and Alexis had wanted to come over today but I just hadn't been up to seeing anybody. So it was quite a shock that C.J. had just shown up at my doorstep.

"Hey, C.J.," I said to him as I stepped into our small living room. C.J. was pacing back and forth. He looked tired and worn out.

"Jasmine, I'm sorry to just drop by like this, but I have really been worried about you. And when Camille, Alexis, and Angel said they hadn't been able to really talk to you, I just couldn't take it anymore. I had to see you," C.J. rambled.

"It's okay. I'm actually glad you came. It means a lot to me." I paused, looking back toward the kitchen where my grandmother was cooking dinner. Everyone else was out, but my grandmother had some supersonic hearing or something so I motioned toward the door. "Let's step outside."

C.J. held the door open as we walked out. He gazed at me, then without saying a word, grabbed me into his arms and just held me. All of the emotions I had bottled up inside me immediately poured out and I cried on his shoulder like a big baby. Surprisingly, I didn't even feel bad or embarrassed about letting him see me in such a horrible condition. It just felt good to have him hug me like that. For just a few minutes, I felt at peace.

He let me cry on his shoulder for a good while before I pulled away.

"How's your mom and the rest of the family doing?"

I sighed. I wasn't sure how my mom was doing. One minute she was the true testament of strength and the next minute she would lose it and burst into tears. I could tell she was trying to be strong for us. But because our walls were paper thin, I could hear her sobbing in her bedroom at night.

"She's taking it real hard," I replied. "And Nikki disappeared to her boyfriend's house after we left the funeral. She's called to check in, but other than that she hasn't really been around. Jalen and Jaheim are really having a hard time. They looked up to Jaquan, so this is really difficult for them." I fought back tears as I thought of my brothers. Jaheim wouldn't stop crying and poor little Jalen had stopped talking altogether. He just sat in a corner and sulked. We'd tried everything, but nothing worked. Even after my grandmother had tried to entice him by offering to let him lick the cake bowl from the chocolate cake she'd made, he still wouldn't say a word.

I was worried about my family, and I guess it showed

on my face because C.J. squeezed my hand and said, "Baby, your family will be okay. And you know if you need anything, I'm here for you."

I nodded, laying my head on his shoulder. He added, "My mom told me to tell you she's praying for you and your family. We all are."

"Thanks," I mumbled. We were going to need a lot of prayer to help us through this.

13

Angel

Today was my first time hanging out since Angelica almost choked to death. I'd gone to Jaquan's funeral and to school, but other than that, I'd spent every moment with my daughter.

I felt awful about everything—giving my baby that candy, almost killing her, then getting so distracted that I wasn't able to warn Jaquan. I'd talked to Miss Rachel and she'd told me over and over that I couldn't blame myself, but still it was hard. My mom, Miss Rachel, and I had gone to the police and I'd told them about what I overheard Al say, but all they would tell me was that they were investigating. I wanted to tell Jasmine so bad, but the police had told us not to say anything because it "would jeopardize their investigation." That was the hardest thing I'd ever had to do, but when that officer told me I could go to jail for obstruction of justice if I said anything, I knew I didn't have any choice.

"So, is shopping making you feel any better?" Camille asked as she browsed the purse rack in Wet Seal.

"I guess so," I replied. I didn't feel right about being away from Angelica, but my mom had insisted I get out of the house while she and Angelica spent the day together. I wanted to say something to Camille about what I knew, but my mom had made me promise to keep quiet because we didn't want anyone from the Blood Brothers finding out I knew anything. I had Angelica to think about, and I couldn't take any chances on somebody doing something to me in retaliation. Plus, my mom had said we didn't know for sure that Al was the one who shot Jaquan. It could've been someone else. My mom convinced me that I had done my part by telling the police what I'd heard, but that didn't make me feel any better.

I walked over to look at an outfit in the window. I picked up the price tag, then quickly let it drop. "Like I really have any money to shop," I mumbled.

I glanced out the window and had to do a double take when I saw one of Camille's ex-boyfriends, Keith. He and two other guys were walking past the window. Camille was too busy looking at a gorgeous pink and green purse to notice. I almost didn't say anything because Keith had been nothing but trouble since the day he came into Ca-mille's life.

When I first met Camille, a judge had sentenced her to the Good Girlz for hiding Keith, then the love of her life, at her grandmother's house. Keith—who had been in jail for carjacking—had failed to tell Camille that he had escaped. She thought that he'd just been released early. Then Keith bailed on her when the cops showed up and Camille was arrested. Her mom hit the roof and forced her to stop talking to him. Although she had moved on, Camille would die if I didn't tell her he was here, so I called out to her.

"Camille, look. There's Keith," I said, pointing out the window.

"Keith who?" she replied, barely looking up from the purse.

"Keith, Keith. Your Keith. Jailbird Keith."

Camille almost broke her neck trying to spot him. As soon as she saw him, she dropped the purse and grabbed my arm, pulling me out of the store.

"Ummmm, I thought we were over him," I urged as we walked quickly to catch up to the group of boys.

She fluffed her spiral curls, pulled down her Soul Sista T, and strutted his way. "I am over him, but I look fabu-lous today, and I want to see him squirm when he sees what he can't have anymore."

Keith and his boys had stopped at one of the shoe stores and were huddled together talking. "Ugggh, he's with his cousin Peanut. I can't stand him," Camille mut-tered. She looked like she was contemplating turning around but Keith spotted her before she could make a move.

"Well, well, well. Looky here. It's the love of my life." He stepped toward Camille, who turned up her top lip in a sneer, even though I could tell she was eating up the attention.

"Whatever, Keith." She folded her arms and looked him up and down. "What's up?"

"It's all you, baby." He returned her stare. "Dang, girl, you look good."

Camille gave him a look as if to say "I know." He finally acknowledged me. "Hey, umm, umm . . ."

"Angel," I said, helping him out.

"Yeah, Angel." He nodded.

"How's your baby?" Camille snidely asked. "And your crazy baby mama?" she added, referring to the mother and child he'd tried to hide from her when they were dating.

"I wanna know how you've been," he said, grinning and trying to look sexy.

Keith and Camille made small talk for a few more minutes. I stood around feeling uncomfortable, not bothering to introduce myself to the broke-down boys who were with him.

One of them, a soulful-looking boy with a fade desperately in need of fading, had just asked me my name, when another guy walked up to them.

"Hey, Larry, what's goin' on, dawg?" the soulful boy said.

"Nothin' much, man," Larry said, giving him some dap. "Just chillin'. You heard the news?"

"What news?" Keith interjected.

"Y'all know that dude who got smoked in Brentwood last month? I think his name was Jaquan."

Both Camille and I turned and stared at him.

"Yeah, I heard about that," Soulful Boy said. "But that's what happens when brothas try to act hard when they ain't. Did they find out who did it?"

The guy named Larry looked around to make sure no one outside our circle was listening. I guess it didn't bother him that Camille and I were there because he talked openly.

"My boy said they arrested this dude named Al, one of the new recruits," the guy said.

"Al Taylor? I know that dude. He goes to the alternative learning center with my little brother," another one of the boys said.

For a minute I felt weak in my knees. I had to hold on to the wall to keep from falling over. I looked over at Camille and she had the exact same look of horror on her face as I did. My head was spinning. Al had been arrested because of me.

"Man, you wanna talk about this later?" Peanut said, nodding in our direction.

They immediately began talking about something else, but I think Camille and I would've been too stunned to listen anyway.

"Ummm, Keith, we gotta go," Camille stammered.

I heard Keith tell her to call him as I scurried off behind her.

"Camille, did you hear that? I can't believe it," I said as

soon as we got out of earshot. "There is absolutely no way this can be true." Somehow, I had been hoping Al didn't do it.

Camille looked shaken. I guess she was thinking the same thing I was—this was going to kill Jasmine. "Maybe it's not true." She didn't give me time to answer as she pulled her cell phone out of her purse.

"Who are you calling?" I asked.

"Alexis," Camille responded. "We have to tell her so we can figure out what to do."

When Camille got Alexis on the phone, she told her what we had heard, and we all decided to meet at Camille's house.

Thirty minutes later we were sitting in Camille's room trying to decide how to tell Jasmine. We knew she was going to have a fit. How was this going to affect her relationship with C.J.? I knew my girl was not going to take this easily. This was one time that Jasmine was really going to need her friends.

We all piled into Alexis's car and headed to Jasmine's apartment. When we got there, no one wanted to get out of the car.

"Okay, guys, we have to go in," Camille said as we sat in the car looking at the apartment complex. "We can do this."

We sighed, climbed out, then made our way up the stairs. Alexis knocked on the door. After a few moments, one of Jasmine's little brothers let us in. He didn't even bother to say hello. He just pointed to the back of the apartment and said, "She's in her room."

I knocked on Jasmine's door and softly called her name. When she didn't answer, I slowly pushed the door open and saw Jasmine lying on her back with her eyes closed. She jumped when she heard the door squeak open.

"Boy, what I tell you about not knocking on my door . . ." Jasmine started fussing before she even opened her eyes. "Oh, hey, y'all. I thought you were one of my annoying little brothers barging in my room again. What are you guys doing here?"

Jasmine rubbed her swollen eyes and sat up on her bed.

"Hey, girl, we just wanted to come by and check on you. Make sure you were okay," Camille said as she hugged Jasmine.

"Sorry for coming by without calling first," Alexis said.

"That's okay. You know y'all are welcome anytime. I need the company."

I took a deep breath before saying, "Jaz, we need to talk to you about something important and we're not sure how you're going to take it."

Jasmine looked at us with a blank expression on her face. "There is nothing you can tell me that will make me feel worse than I already do."

"Well now, I don't know about that," Alexis mumbled.

I shot her a look before continuing. "Camille and I were at the mall today and we saw Keith. You know, Camille's ex, Keith?" Jasmine looked at me as if to say

"Hurry up with the story." "Well, some guy came up to him and some of his friends talking about what happened to Jaquan," I continued.

At the mention of her brother's name, Jasmine's expression quickly turned serious. "And?"

"Well, anyway, the boy said that they made an arrest in the case," I continued.

"What? Who? When? I can't believe it. Why hadn't someone told us? Wait 'til I tell Mama." She was already swinging her legs over the side of the bed.

"Hold up, Jasmine." Camille stopped her. "Before you go say anything, let us finish." Camille took a deep breath and continued. "One of the boys said that they had arrested Al."

"Al who?" Jasmine asked, confused.

"C.J.'s brother, Al," I gently said. I still felt bad. I didn't know if I could ever tell her—or anybody other than Miss Rachel for that matter—that I'd known what Al was planning before he actually went through with it. If I told Jasmine, I knew that she would never forgive me.

Her mouth dropped open but no words came out. "No way. You are lying to me," she finally said, her eyes darting from me to Camille, then to Alexis. "Please tell me you are lying." The looks on our faces must've told her we were serious because she groaned and collapsed back onto the bed.

"Jasmine, I hope to God it's not true, but we had to tell you what we heard," Camille said consolingly.

"Maybe you heard wrong." Jasmine reached for the

phone. "I'm going to call C.J. so he can clear this up."

None of us said anything as she dialed C.J.'s number. I know we all were hoping C.J. would tell her it was just a big misunderstanding. But something in my gut told me that wouldn't be the case.

14

Jasmine

I prayed as I dialed C.J.'s cell phone number. My hand was shaking so bad, it took me three tries to get the number right. *Dear God, please let this be a mistake.*

C.J. answered his cell phone on the second ring. His voice sounded heavy, like he was really tired.

"Hello," he said.

"C.J., tell me it's not true!" I said, skipping the greetings.

"Jasmine? Wh-what are you talkin' about?"

"Your brother," I shouted, my chest starting to heave up and down. "Please tell me your brother isn't the one who shot Jaquan."

His silence spoke volumes. Camille, Angel, and Alexis moved in and sat next to me on the bed.

"C.J., did Al do it?" I repeated, my words coming out slower.

"Jasmine, I'm so sorry," C.J. said. He sounded hoarse.

I could not believe this. "Why didn't you say something?" I screamed. "How long have you known?"

He hesitated before saying, "Yesterday."

"Yesterday!" I yelled. "Why didn't you call me right away?"

"Jasmine, I didn't know what to say. This all has come as a shock to me, too. All I know is one minute I'm at home having dinner with my family, the next the cops are kicking in my door. My mom is about to lose her mind."

"Your mom?" I cried. "What about my mom? What about my entire family? We lost my brother and now you're telling me your brother is the one responsible?"

"Jasmine, calm down," C.J. said.

I was just about to reply when I turned to see my sister standing in the doorway. Her eyes were wide in horror.

"I gotta go," I said, slamming the phone down before he could say another word.

"Tell me I did not just hear what I thought I heard," Nikki said, her eyes brimming with tears.

"Why are you eavesdropping on me?"

She didn't take her eyes off me. "It's my room, too. Answer me."

Camille, Alexis, and Angel stood up. "Jaz, we're gonna go. Call us if you need us."

Angel hugged me. "No matter what time, we're here for you."

They all looked at me sadly before leaving without even speaking to Nikki.

After they'd gone, Nikki demanded, "Answer me, Jasmine. Did your little bootleg boyfriend have something to do with Jaquan's death?"

I ignored her dig at C.J. and replied, "*He* didn't. But apparently his brother did."

"How do you know this?" she said, narrowing her eyes.

"Angel and Camille overheard someone talking about it today and told me. So I called C.J."

"And he confirmed it?" she asked, her voice shaky.

I nodded, suddenly getting an uneasy feeling. "Yeah, C.J. said the cops just burst into—"

Nikki didn't give me time to finish. She turned and bolted from the room. I knew exactly where she was headed when I heard her screaming, "Mama! Maaaama!"

I followed Nikki down the hall, trying desperately to convince her to let me be the one to tell Mama.

"Nikki, stop!"

Both my grandmother and my mother came racing out of their room. "Good Lord, girl. What are you runnin' around here yellin' for? Is something on fire?" my grandmother asked.

"Granny," Nikki said, getting hysterical. I didn't know if she was being her usual drama queen self or if she really was that upset. "Jas-Jasmine's boyfriend's brother. Th-They've arrested him for shooting Jaquan."

"What?" my mother gasped, looking at me.

"Jasmine, what happened?" my grandmother demanded, pulling her housecoat belt tightly around her waist.

"Why didn't the police call us and tell us they'd arrested someone?" my mother said, leaning against the wall to steady herself.

"Jasmine, answer me," my grandmother demanded.

By this point, Jalen and Jaheim had come out into the hallway as well. I watched as all eyes turned my way. And as I began relaying what I had just found out, the horror across my family members' faces let me know that our troubles were nowhere near over.

15

Jasmine

Trouble had just landed on my doorstep. That's all that went through my mind as I looked at C.J. standing outside my front door, a pitiful expression on his face.

Why in the world would he show up here? No, I knew why. He'd been calling me all day, and I refused to take his calls. I just needed some time to process everything. I never expected him to show up here.

"Can I help you?" Nikki snapped at him. She'd been the one to open the front door. I was sitting in the living room with her and my brothers watching TV. My grandmother was at church and my mom was in the back taking a nap.

"Ummm, can I talk to Jasmine?" C.J. said, shifting uncomfortably.

"No, you can't," she said, folding her arms across her chest. "Go talk to your thug brother."

C.J. took a deep breath. "Please."

"Don't nobody care 'bout you beggin'."

I walked over to the door. "Nikki, I got this."

She cut her eyes at me, then turned and stormed down the hallway. I knew she was heading straight to my mom's room.

"C.J., you need to leave," I said quickly.

"Just let me talk to you for a minute."

"Your brother killed my brother!" I looked down to see a teary-eyed Jalen standing next to me, wearing a scowl.

"Little man, I'm so sorry about what happened," C.J. said. From the sorrowful look on his face, you'd have thought he was the one who shot Jaquan.

"For real, C.J., you need to go," I said, glancing toward my mom's bedroom.

"But, Jasmine, this isn't fair. Let me just talk . . ." His words trailed off as he turned his attention to my mother, who was now standing in the middle of the living room. Like Jalen, she wore a scowl, only hers looked twice as mean. Nikki was standing behind her looking like a guard dog.

"Ms. Jones, I am so sorry. My family is so sorry. We just—"

"I cannot believe you would show your face here," she said.

I don't know why, but I felt the need to come to his defense. "Mama, he just came to offer his condolences. He's not staying."

"I know he's not," she growled. "What kind of monster did your parents raise?"

The question seemed to catch C.J. off guard.

"Ms. Jones, Al, he . . . he really isn't that bad."

I grimaced because I knew my mom was about to go off. As I expected, she said, "Not that bad? Not that bad? My child is dead because of him and you want to tell me how your brother isn't that bad?"

"But—"

My mom took a deep breath. "Little boy, get away from the door. Stay away from my daughter and stay out of our lives!"

C.J. looked like he was fighting off tears, but he didn't say anything. He just turned and walked away. And as I closed the door behind him, I cried for us both. My mother glared at me, then turned and walked back to her room.

16

Angel

I know I said I was going to leave Marcus alone, but the whole situation with Angelica choking and losing Jaquan had made me want to try one more time. It hadn't helped that today Angelica called the mailman daddy. I hated that, but since he was the only male she saw on a regular basis, she must've gotten confused.

The mailman had laughed and ruffled her curly hair, but after he left I tried to explain to her that he wasn't her daddy. Then she said, "Where my dad-dee?" and I wanted to cry.

I immediately marched back into the house. I sat in the living room and called Marcus.

"What up?" he said, answering on the first ring. I'd blocked my number just so he wouldn't recognize it.

"Marcus?"

He was silent. I wanted to go off, but I decided that's where I went wrong last time.

"It's Angel," I said when he didn't respond. "I need to talk to you."

A pause, then, "About what?"

I glanced over at Angelica, who was sucking on her sippy cup and dozing off.

"I don't have any money," he said, breaking the silence.

So what else is new? "I didn't call you for money," I finally answered. As bad as I needed it, that's not what this conversation was about.

"Well, what is it?"

"Angelica. She wants to know where her daddy is and why he won't come see her." So maybe she hadn't said that latter part, but I threw it in for good measure. Maybe if I could tug at Marcus's emotions, he'd come around, be a part of her life, and maybe even give us some money.

Silence filled the line again.

"Angelica, sh-she almost died. She choked the other day, and well, it just scared me and then today, she asked about you, and well, I just thought about the fact that life is too precious." That sounded just like something my mom would say, but it was the truth.

"What do you mean she almost died?" he asked almost frantically. For the first time since he'd found out about Angelica, Marcus seemed genuinely concerned. "What kind of mother are you? Weren't you watching her?"

Okay, so much for being nice. No, he wasn't trying to get on me about my parenting skills.

"I'm a parent who's here," I snapped, "which is more than I can say for you."

"What if something had happened to her?" he snapped back.

"Now you care?" I had to stop myself and take a deep breath. "Look, don't try to talk about how I'm raising our daughter, because at least I didn't abandon her."

"What do you want, Angel?" he huffed.

"I want you to see your daughter. Are you so coldhearted that you don't care about that beautiful little girl?"

When he didn't say anything, I continued. "You know what? Forget it, Marcus. I tried. I'm done. I'm sorry I bothered you." I slammed the phone down. I knew calling Marcus would be hard, I just had no idea it would hurt like this. But I had to finally accept the fact that Marcus was not going to be a part of my daughter's life.

I had just buried my face in my hands when I felt a hand gently touch my shoulders.

"Mija?"

I turned around to face my mother, and before I could open my mouth, I burst into tears.

I must've cried for ten minutes while my mother held me and rubbed my hair. Finally, I pulled myself together. "How long were you standing there? I thought you were in the back asleep."

"I was. And I've been here long enough to hear everything." She stroked my cheek. "My precious baby girl. Forced to grow up so soon."

I sniffed. My mother was right. I should be worried about history tests and what I was going to wear to the next big party, not child support and trifling baby daddies.

"You young girls today, you don't realize what a gift you have," my mother continued, shaking her head sadly. Her eyes suddenly lit up as she jumped up and walked over to get her purse, which sat in a chair by the front door. She reached in the purse, pulled out a hundred-dollar bill, and handed it to me.

I took the money, confused. "What's this for?"

My mother folded her arms. "What could Marcus say to you to get you to give him that hundred dollars?"

I raised my eyebrows. "Huh?"

"What could he say to you to get that money?"

I glanced down at the hundred-dollar bill. "Absolutely nothing. I can't stand him."

"What about before you started hating him?"

"Even then. He couldn't have gotten this. This is a lot of money." I was so not understanding what her point was.

"So, could any boy talk that money away from you?"

"No way."

My mother's eyes softened as I sat back down on the sofa. "*Mija,* you don't think you're worth more than a hundred dollars?" She covered my hands with her own.

"Of course I am."

"Then why did you let Marcus talk you out of something worth so much more than this hundred-dollar bill?"

I was speechless as her words set in. My mom always

could say deep stuff that really hit home. I used to not listen to her, but this time, I heard her loud and clear.

"Angel, I'm not saying this to beat you up. What's done is done, but I want you to understand for the future. Guard the gift that God gave you."

I slowly nodded. "But what am I supposed to do about Marcus?"

"Turn him over to God. Pray that he comes around, then release your worries. Yes, Angelica needs her father, but we have more than enough love to give her."

As if on cue, Angelica squirmed.

"Your baby's waking up," my mother said. "Time to give her a bath."

My mother headed back to her bedroom, then stopped and walked back over to me. I actually enjoyed these mother-daughter moments now, and I know she did, too. I figured she had just come back to give me a hug or something. Instead, she reached down and pulled the hundred-dollar bill from my hand. "I know you didn't think you were keeping that."

I smiled for the first time that day.

17

Jasmine

I had thought Jaquan's funeral was hard. This was just as difficult.

I'd never been inside a courtroom, but it looked just like it did on TV shows. A United States flag hung on the dull brown panel behind the silver-haired judge. He was a big man and looked mean as all get-out. I wouldn't ever want to go in front of him for anything.

I glanced back at my girls. Camille, Angel, and Alexis gave me reassuring smiles. It felt good to have them here—I needed their support. I even let out a small smile when I saw Miss Rachel sitting in the row behind them.

My mom was sitting next to me. My grandmother and I had to hold her up, because she kept silently crying and slumping over. It seemed like she hadn't stopped crying since she found out Al was behind the shooting. It was heartbreaking to see my mother, who was usually so strong, so weak and helpless.

Jaheim, Jalen, and Nikki sat on the other side of me. We were all in the second row, waiting to see the boy who had killed our brother.

I peeked over at C.J., who was wiping his eyes. He was sitting with his family on the opposite side of the courtroom. His mom was crying, too. Even his dad was red-eyed. They'd approached us right before court and had tried to apologize profusely for Al's actions, but my mother wouldn't hear it. She'd scowled at them and walked into the courtroom without acknowledging their apology.

C.J. caught me staring at him. He looked like he wanted to say something to me, but I quickly turned my head away because I didn't want to give my mom any reason to go off.

The district attorney had called us the same night we found out about Al and told us about the arrest. He said Al's attorney had requested bail, so that's why we were in court this morning.

"Are we ready to begin?" the judge asked.

The prosecutor, who had filled us in on how everything would go down, stood up. "We are, Your Honor."

The judge motioned for the bailiff to bring out Al. It seemed like it took forever, but according to my Hello Kitty watch, it was only a couple of minutes before the deputy led Al out.

He was dressed in a bright orange jumpsuit with black

numbers across the back. He had shackles around his legs and arms, which made him scoot when he walked. His hair was unbraided and wild and he looked scared. C.J.'s mom let out a loud sob when she saw him.

"What is she crying for?" my mother mumbled, clutching her tissue. "At least she can see her son."

Al scooted in front of the judge, and some overweight man in a too-small tan suit walked up next to him.

"Your Honor, my client has never been in any kind of trouble. He comes from a good, decent Christian family and is not a flight risk, so therefore we respectfully request that he be released on bail."

"Are you crazy?" my mother shouted, jumping up. My grandmother grabbed her arm just as the judge shot her an admonishing look.

"Shhh, Jetola, let the law handle this," my grandmother warned.

My mother snatched her arm away but sat back down.

"Your Honor," the prosecutor began, "we strongly object to the granting of bail for this man. He opened fire on a crowded basketball court and callously shot down a fifteen-year-old basketball star, who was already receiving scholarship offers to college. He ended the life of a young man who, despite his circumstances, was heading places."

"I was just trying to scare him," Al whimpered. "I didn't mean—"

"Mr. Vanderburg," the judge interrupted, "I would advise you to remind your client that he is not to speak unless I ask him to. And while you're reminding him of that, please remind him that when you pull out a gun in a crowd of people, I don't buy that you have no intention of using it."

"Yes, Your Honor," Mr. Vanderburg said. "But please understand that my client was under pressure from local gangs—"

"Let me cut you off, Mr. Vanderburg," the judge said. "Thousands of young boys—who don't come from such decent Christian households—walk away from the pressures of gangs every single day." The judge turned his attention to Al. "Where's your gang now? Are any of them in this courtroom with you? Are any of them facing life in prison with you?"

I could tell the judge was getting disgusted. The prosecutor had told us earlier that we lucked out getting this particular judge because he couldn't stand gangs and, in fact, had started some type of community task force to fight the growing gang problem.

"And furthermore, if you do come from such a good family, what were you doing in a gang in the first place?" the judge continued. I wanted to know the answer to that one myself.

Al just lowered his head. Both of his parents, as well as C.J. and Cynthia, were crying hard.

The judge shook his head as he turned toward the prosecutor. "However, since Mr. Taylor is a juvenile, with no record, I will grant bail, at two hundred and fifty thousand dollars. Court is adjourned." He pounded his gavel at the same time my mother let out a scream.

"No!"

Watching my mother get hysterical brought tears to my eyes.

C.J. looked at me as his parents comforted each other. Our eyes met and I could tell he was thinking the same thing that I was—even if we did want to work things out, there was no way we'd ever be able to get past this.

18

Jasmine

I stared at the big D– and *See me* plastered across the top of my history paper. Mrs. Reed had handed me the paper as I left her class. I think she wanted me to talk to her then, but luckily, another teacher came in and started chatting, so I made my escape. I wasn't in the mood to deal with Mrs. Reed and have her get all on me for the half-done paper. Shoot, I wasn't in the mood for much of anything lately.

"What happened to you yesterday? You missed the Good Girlz meeting," Camille asked, showing up beside my locker.

I stuffed the paper inside my locker. "I just wasn't up for it."

"Well, you know we had that mentoring session. Me, Alexis, and Angel had to pick up the slack, and you know Miss Rachel wasn't happy."

"Look, I just couldn't make it, okay?" I slammed my locker shut.

Camille held up her hands. "Dang, calm down. I was just asking."

I turned around and leaned against the locker. "Sorry. My life is just turned upside down. My house is like a morgue. Everybody's walking around not saying anything. C.J. is blowing up my phone, and I just want everything to return to normal."

"I'm sorry, Jaz," she said. "But can I ask you something?"

"Can I stop you?"

She smiled. "Not really. Are you being fair to C.J.? I mean, it's not really his fault."

I let out a frustrated sigh. "I know it isn't. But he still could've told me about his brother. I wonder if he would have ever said anything if I hadn't found out."

"Come on. You know him better than that."

"Just drop it, Camille, because even if I did want to forgive him, my mom is so not trying to hear that."

"Okay, I'll leave it alone." She pointed toward the cafeteria. "Are you going in to eat?"

"No, I just kinda feel like being by myself." Before I could say anything else, my day went from bad to worse as Tori stopped in front of my locker. As usual, her cheerleader flunkies stood behind her. Even though I couldn't stand her, I had to admit that she was pretty, although

I'd never ever tell her that. Tori was about five-five, size six, with long, beautiful jet-black hair, and was a lovely chocolate color.

"Jasmine, I hadn't had a chance to tell you I'm so sorry to hear what happened to your brother. And I'm really sorry to hear that C.J.'s brother did it." She put her hand to her chest like she was shocked.

"Tori, don't talk to me," I said.

Tori turned up her nose. "Look, I'm trying to be nice to you." She turned to her friends. "Some people you just can't be nice to."

"Tori, go away," Camille said. "Please."

"Whatever." She glanced down the hall and spotted C.J. walking toward us. "I'll go away. Maybe C.J. will be more receptive to my sympathy." She strutted off, heading straight toward C.J.

Camille quickly put her hand on my arm. "Come on, Jaz. You know she's just trying to get to you."

I watched as Tori openly flirted with C.J. He obviously was trying to go around her, but she literally was blocking his path.

"I gotta go," I said. "I'll talk to you later."

"Jasmine! Wait up!" C.J. called out. I don't know how he got Tori to move, but I didn't turn around to find out.

I had just made it outside into the courtyard when C.J. caught up with me. "Jasmine, how long are you going to ignore me?"

I stopped and spun around. "What part of 'leave me alone' don't you get?"

"You don't mean that. I know you don't. I'm sorry

about what happened to your brother. And I don't understand how my brother got caught up in a gang. But that shouldn't affect our relationship."

"You knew he was messing with that gang," I said. "Why didn't you do anything?" I knew I was lashing out, but I was hurting and I just wanted the pain to go away.

"Don't you think I ask myself that every day?" C.J. said. "Yeah, Al may be out on bail, but he's walking around like a zombie, devastated about what happened. My whole family is falling apart."

I glared at him through tear-filled eyes. "You don't know what falling apart is."

He reached out and gently touched my arm. "Jasmine, don't shut me out."

I snatched my arm away. "C.J., for the last time, leave me alone." I said it, but my heart didn't feel it. And I think C.J. knew that. Still, he nodded.

"Fine. I'll leave you alone. For now. But you and me, we ain't over. I'm going to keep trying." He turned and walked off.

I glanced over at the sign posted outside our school. It read WE'LL MISS YOU, JAQUAN.

C.J.'s words rang in my ears. *We ain't over.* In my heart, I knew we weren't; I just didn't have any idea how we'd get over this.

19

Angel

"This is tight!" I stared at the picture of Jaquan clutching a basketball. It was from the school yearbook and it was one of the nicest photos of Jaquan I'd ever seen. I didn't know what Camille wanted it for when she asked me to get it from the teacher in charge of the yearbook, but now, looking at it in the black and gold frame, I was glad my friend was so creative.

Camille had framed the picture, then wrote an original poem called "Gone Too Soon." She'd printed the poem out and put it in the frame as well.

"You like?" Camille said.

"I love," I replied. "Girl, you are so talented."

Camille smiled as if to say "I know."

"So when are we gonna give it to Jasmine?" I asked.

"Well, I figured we could go by her house this evening and give it to her. I already sent Alexis a text. She's picking us up after school." Jasmine had missed school today. I know she was still broken up about her brother, and having to come here and see C.J. wasn't making it any easier.

"Cool, I'll see you then."

After school we met Alexis and made our way over to Jasmine's. We all felt awful and wanted to do something to cheer her up. No one knew it, but I felt the worst of all, although I was trying to take Miss Rachel's advice and not blame myself for what happened to Jaquan.

"Hello, Ms. Jones," we said when Jasmine's mother answered the door. "We're here to see Jasmine."

Her mother forced a smile as she said, "Come on in."

Jasmine was in the living room, staring blankly at the television. I knew she wasn't watching, because the TV was on *Jeopardy!* and in her right mind, Jasmine wouldn't have been caught dead watching *Jeopardy!*

"Hey, Jaz," we all said as we walked in.

"Hey," she said. I wanted to cry. It was like something had sucked the life out of the entire apartment.

"We were just worried about you and wanted to come by and check on you," Camille said.

"Thanks, but I'm fine," Jasmine replied. "I just didn't feel like going to school today and my mom said it was okay for me to stay home."

"Hello, girls," Jasmine's grandmother said, appearing in the doorway. "I'm glad you came. Jasmine can use some company." She sighed heavily. "I would offer you some food, but I didn't cook anything today."

Okay, now I *knew* sadness had taken over the household. Jasmine's grandmother not cooking? That was unheard of.

"No, we're good," Alexis said.

"Why don't you take the girls on back into your room, Jasmine?" her grandmother asked.

Jasmine had just stood up to lead us back when there was a knock on the door. I was closest to the door, so I said, "I'll get it."

I looked out the peephole and froze.

"Well, who is it?" Jasmine asked.

I glanced around the room. All eyes were on me. I didn't know what to say. Finally, Jasmine marched over to the door and swung it open.

I heard Jasmine's mother take a sharp breath when she saw C.J. standing on her doorstep.

"I-I'm so sorry for coming over. But I was really worried and y-you're not answering the phone," C.J. said.

By this time, Jasmine's mother had stood and walked over to the door. "You're one hardheaded little boy, ain't you?"

"Ms. Jones, you have to know, my whole family is sorry," C.J. began.

"And you have to know that I could care less how your whole family is feeling."

"C.J., why are you here?" Jasmine finally said.

He finally held out an envelope. "My family, we just wanted to give you this."

Jasmine took it. "What is this?" she said, opening it. C.J. didn't reply as she pulled out a check.

"Ten thousand dollars?" Jasmine said. "What is this for?"

Jasmine's mother walked over and snatched the check away. "What is this?" she said, staring at the check. "So your family thinks they can just pay us off and everything will be fine? Is this what my son is worth to you, ten thousand dollars?" She waved the check in his face.

"N-no, ma'am," C.J. stuttered. "We're not trying to put a price on him. It's just that my mother—we all—felt so bad that we wanted to give you something to help with the funeral costs."

Jasmine's mother tore up the check and tossed it in C.J.'s face. "Tell your family we're not for sale." She spun around and marched toward her bedroom, stopping just before she got to the hallway. "Y'all need to be using the money for a therapist, so you can figure out why my son, despite his surroundings"—she motioned around her—"was heading places. And your brother, despite your money and your two-parent household, hooked up with a gang that turned him into a murderer."

C.J. looked stung by the words, but he just stood there.

Jasmine's grandmother stepped toward her daughter. "Jetola, you're upset. Don't do this."

"You're doggone right I'm upset," she said, pulling away from her mother and walking back over to C.J. I could tell she was getting angrier by the minute. "Every statistic out there said my boy wouldn't make it. And he *was* making it.

He was gonna be somebody, and his brother"—she jabbed C.J. in the chest—"with his privileged lifestyle, took that away."

The whole scene was heartbreaking. Jasmine had started crying again. Her mom seemed on the verge of losing it, and poor C.J. looked like he wished he could disappear.

"Get out!" Jasmine's mom hissed.

"But, Ms. Jones—" C.J. tried to say.

"Get out now!"

"Baby, it's best that you leave and don't come back," Jasmine's grandmother gently said to C.J. as she once again pulled at her daughter. "I know your intentions are good, but our family isn't ready for this."

Jasmine was now crying so hard that both Camille and Alexis were hugging her tightly.

C.J. looked at Jasmine, tears filling his eyes. "I'm sorry." Then he turned his attention back to Jasmine's mother. "I'm really sorry. We all are."

As I watched C.J. leave, I couldn't help wrapping my arms around Jasmine, too. Our friend was going to need us now more than ever.

20

Angel

*M*y heart went out to C.J. He was all choked up as he sat in the back of the restaurant. He had called Camille, Alexis, and me and asked us to meet him at Chili's restaurant because he really needed to talk. I could see how torn up he was about the entire situation. I couldn't imagine how he must have been feeling, knowing his brother had killed his girlfriend's brother.

"Thank you for agreeing to meet with me," C.J. said to us in a very shaky voice. "I just really needed to talk to someone. I don't know what else to do. It's been a week since that blowup at her apartment and Jasmine still won't answer my calls. She won't even look at me at school. And she even gave me back the iPod and bracelet I gave her for Valentine's Day."

Camille turned to C.J. "C.J., you have to understand how Jasmine feels. How her whole family feels. Losing Jaquan was really hard on them."

"I know, but it wasn't my fault. I understand that it was because of one of my family members, but I just want to be there for her. I mean, if you think about it, in a way I'm losing a brother, too. Al is probably going to get life for killing Jaquan. I know there is no comparison, but it still hurts. What can I do?"

We all looked at one another. I wasn't quite sure what to tell him. While I understood and sympathized with C.J., I also understood how hard this must be on Jasmine. I was torn. I didn't know what to tell him. I know that C.J. was sincere, but my loyalties lay with Jasmine, and she'd made it clear that it was over between her and C.J.

"C.J., this is hard on all of us," Alexis said. "You are just going to have to give Jasmine and her family some time to heal. They just buried Jaquan a few weeks ago. I'm sure after a little while she'll want to talk to you."

"You don't understand," C.J. said a little too loudly. "I don't have time. I am losing my mind not being able to talk to her. Jasmine had become one of my best friends. She is just as important to me as she is to you. I want to help her get through this just like I need her to help me get through it."

We all looked at C.J. as tears began to fall freely from his eyes. I had never seen a guy actually cry over a girl, so it was a shock to me.

"C.J., please don't cry," I said. "Maybe we can talk to her for you. I mean, I don't know if it will help, but we can try."

C.J.'s eyes briefly lit up. "Will you please do that for me? I normally wouldn't put you girls in the middle of this, but I have no other choice at this point. Can you just tell her how much I am hurting, too? I want her to know that I need to hear her voice. Just let her know that I apologize on behalf of my family. My mom is so torn up about this that she won't even get out of bed."

I looked at Camille and Alexis, and they both nodded.

"Okay, thank you so much." He stood and pulled out some money to pay for our food.

After he left, we sat and continued talking.

"I don't know what we should do," I finally said.

"Honestly, I feel like a traitor already just having this conversation," Alexis said. "We're supposed to be on Jasmine's side."

Camille shook her head. "Alexis, there is no side to be on. As Jasmine's best friends we need to do what's right and what's best for her. And I think what's best for her is to help her to see that this is not C.J.'s fault. Eventually she is going to need to start the road to healing, and that road starts with C.J. She and her family are going to have to learn to forgive in order to move on with their lives. Isn't that what Miss Rachel is always teaching us?"

"I agree," I said, taking a sip of my strawberry smoothie. "But how are we going to get her to see that without pushing her away? Shoot, she just started really opening up to us, and you know Jasmine ain't even tryin' to hear forgive and forget."

"Well," Camille said, finally smiling. "We are just going to have to get creative. We're all too young to be dealin' with such deep stuff, so it's up to us to bring some happiness back in the Good Girlz' world."

I was definitely with that. I was willing to try anything to lift the dark cloud that hung over us.

21

Jasmine

"Okay, who wants to open up the meeting tonight with a quick prayer?" Miss Rachel asked as we sat in a circle at our weekly Good Girlz meeting.

"I will," Camille responded almost too quickly. Miss Rachel usually had to dang near pull someone's teeth to get them to lead the prayer. I should have known that something was up, since all my friends kept nervously looking at one another. Still, I was truly touched when Camille made a point to say a prayer for me and my family.

This was my first meeting since Al's hearing, and it felt really good to be back around my friends and not have to think about the entire situation. Things had really been tense at my house since Al's hearing. My mom couldn't stop ranting about how she couldn't believe Al was out on bail. And it seemed like she was reminding me every other minute to "stay away from C.J."

As we finished praying, I cleared my throat to speak. "Before we get started I wanted to say something. Y'all know I'm not a touchy-feely kind of girl, but I have to share something with all of you. I really wanted to say thank you to each of you, and to you, too, Miss Rachel. With everything going on with my family, you guys have been so supportive. I've never had a close relationship with my sister, so your love and support means a lot to me."

"I hope she's still saying that after this meeting is over," Angel whispered to Camille. I guess she thought I couldn't hear her. I was just about to ask her what that meant when Alexis interjected.

"Girl, you know we love you, too. Now can we stop all this mushy talk? I just did my makeup and I'm not trying to mess it up with crying."

We all laughed. Leave it to Alexis to be worried about her makeup. We went on to talk about our next upcoming service project when there was a knock at the door. The looks on my friends' faces told me that whoever was on the other side of that door was someone I wasn't going to be happy to see. Angel, Camille, and Alexis all looked like they were afraid to move.

"What's wrong with y'all?" I asked. "You look like you've seen a . . ." They all put their heads down as I stopped in midsentence when I saw C.J. poke his head in the door.

"Can I come in?" he asked.

"What is *he* doing here?" I said through clenched teeth.

"Jasmine, before you go off, just hear him out, *please*," Camille pleaded.

"You mean to tell me that y'all *knew* he was coming here tonight? I can't believe this!" I snapped. "You guys are supposed to be my best friends."

"Jasmine, they are," C.J. said as he walked all the way into the room. He looked as cute as ever in a maroon sweater vest over a beige polo and faded jeans. But I wasn't going to be swayed by his cuteness.

"Who asked you?"

Angel stammered, "W-we just want to see you happy. We did this for you."

"Please don't be mad at them," C.J. said, stepping closer to me. "This was all my idea. I had to find a way to see you so we could talk."

"Talk! Talk about what? You should've been talkin' to me about your brother! We have nothing to say to each other. I thought I told you I didn't want to see you anymore. We're over." I was so angry I thought I was going to lose it.

"Jasmine, listen to me. You have to find a way to heal. To move on. Life is too short," Camille tried to reason. "Take it from someone who knows." Camille had lost her father a couple of years ago, and her mother had almost died of a heart attack last year. She'd blamed herself because she'd been causing her mom all kinds of stress.

Miss Rachel walked over to me and touched me lightly on the shoulder. "Jasmine, she's right."

"Not you, too, Miss Rachel. You knew about this, too?" I couldn't take it anymore. I shook my head at them as I stood up and ran from the room. I rushed into the ladies' room and locked myself in a stall. After a few minutes, I heard the door creak open.

"Jasmine," I heard Miss Rachel say as she quietly closed the door behind her.

"Miss Rachel, I don't want to talk about it. Just leave me alone, please." I was trippin'. Part of me just wanted C.J. to hug me real tight but the other part knew I had to get over him.

"No, I won't leave you alone," Rachel said. "I've known you since you were two years old, and I've seen you make too much progress to watch you go back inside your shell. Now, whether you want to hear it or not, you are going to listen to me. So, you can choose to listen through this restroom door or you can come out here and talk to me like the mature young lady I know you are."

I don't know how she does it, but Miss Rachel always has a way of getting me to do what she wants. I slowly opened the stall door and came out. She was standing there with open arms. I walked into her arms and let out all the tears I had been holding in. I was scared because I wanted to be with C.J., but it just didn't seem right.

"Miss Rachel, I'm so confused. This is so hard on me. I care a whole lot about C.J., and I know this isn't his fault, but I owe my family some type of loyalty, don't I?"

Miss Rachel pulled back and took my face in her hands. "Jasmine, look at me. I know that a tragedy has happened to your family, and you have every right to be angry. But, don't let that anger destroy you. And that's what you are doing by continuing to place blame. Don't you know that everything that happens, happens for a reason? Maybe God needed your brother in Heaven. Whatever the reason, you will never be happy if you don't make peace with this situation, and that is going to start when you talk to that young man in there who seems to care for you very deeply." Rachel wiped my tears. "Now, you know I don't condone you girls getting so serious so soon, but if you have to be serious with someone, C.J. is the perfect candidate."

A thin smile crossed my face as I decided to go ahead and hear C.J. out. I guess it really couldn't hurt. Miss Rachel and I walked back to the room to find the rest of the girls all sitting around C.J., trying to console him. There wasn't a dry eye in the room.

C.J. looked up and saw me and immediately stood up. "Jasmine, can we please talk?"

"Ladies, let's finish our meeting in my office and give these two a chance to talk in private," Miss Rachel said.

After everyone left the room, I turned my attention to C.J. "Okay, I'm listening."

"Jasmine, I can't say I'm sorry enough for what my brother did. If I could take it back I would. And I'm sorry I didn't tell you the minute I found out. I know none of this is going to bring Jaquan back, but we have to find a way to get on with our lives. And I can't get on with my life without you in it. I feel like I'm dying inside," C.J. pleaded as tears flowed freely from his eyes.

He looks so doggone cute right now, tears and all. I had never had a guy cry in front of me, so this was new to me. Any other guy crying in front of me, I probably would've thought was weak, but there was something so real about C.J.'s tears that I didn't see it as weakness at all.

"C.J., I just don't know what to think right now. I know this isn't your fault, but because of one of your family members, I will never see my brother again. I owe my family some loyalty. My mom would die if she knew I even was talking to you right now."

C.J. looked down and shook his head. "Let me talk to her. I'll do whatever it takes to make things better. I love you, so this has to work out."

Did he just say "I love you"? I really must be hearing things.

"What did you just say?" I mumbled. "Because it sounded like you said 'I love you.' "

"I did." He looked at me, his eyes letting me know he was telling the truth. "I mean, I have never felt this way about a girl. I can't function if I'm not able to talk to you."

My jaw almost hit the floor. I couldn't believe C.J. actually told me he loved me. Yes, we were serious about each other but we'd never said the "L" word. Wait 'til I tell my friends. At that point, I was convinced. I couldn't let go of C.J. He was too important to lose. Plus, I was going to need his support to make it through the next few months.

"I love you, too, C.J." I smiled through my tears.

"Then can we please figure out a way together to convince our families that it's okay for us to be together?"

I nodded as he pulled me to him and hugged me tightly.

I welcomed his hug, but I think we both knew that making my family okay with our relationship wasn't going to be as easy as we hoped.

22

Jasmine

It felt like old times. C.J. and I were at the movies, where we'd just finished watching Tyler Perry's new movie. It felt so good to have things return to normal. I had been apprehensive about meeting him tonight. I wasn't sure I was ready to go out in public and chance being seen. But we'd come to a movie theater way across town, and I was really glad I did come.

Now we were on our way next door to Baskin-Robbins for ice cream. My mom thought I was at Camille's house studying. I didn't like lying to her, but I knew there was no way she'd ever let me see C.J., so I had to do what I had to do.

At Baskin-Robbins we both ordered a cone of vanilla

with sprinkles. I thought C.J. looked so cute eating his ice cream, it made me smile.

"What do you want to do now?" C.J. asked as we walked back to his car.

"I don't know. What do you want to do?"

"Anything but take you back to Camille's. I'm not ready for this night to end," he softly said. "I missed you so much, Jasmine."

I smiled. "I missed you, too, C.J."

My eyes slowly closed as he leaned in to kiss me. My heart had started fluttering in anticipation when I heard someone shout, "Oh, no, you didn't!"

My eyes shot open as I looked for the source of the voice. My ears weren't deceiving me. That was my sister, standing right in front of me with her hands planted firmly on her hips. I wanted to die. Of all the people to bump into, it had to be my sister. She was with her equally ghetto girlfriend, Uniqua.

"Nikki, what are you doin' here?"

"The question is, what are *you* doin' here?" she asked, her nose turned up as she looked C.J. up and down. "And with *him*."

"I'm minding my business," I said casually, thinking maybe if I acted like it was no big deal, she wouldn't trip.

No such luck. "With this freak? Oh no, wait 'til Mama hears you're out here all hugged up with the enemy. The fool who got your brother shot."

"Come on, Nikki."

C.J. lowered his eyes, not saying anything.

"Dang, he's the reason Jaquan got shot?" Uniqua asked as she smacked on a mouthful of gum.

"He sho' is," Nikki said, her voice laced with disgust. "Well, he didn't do it, but his brother did."

"His *brother*," I reminded Nikki. "C.J. didn't have anything to do with it."

"Whatever. Tell it to Mama," Nikki said, stomping off.

"Nikki, wait," I called after her.

She gave me the hand as she walked away, her ghetto friend right behind her.

"Oh, dang," I said, falling back against the car.

"I'm so sorry. I didn't mean to get you in trouble," C.J. said. "I just wanted to spend time with you."

I looked at him. His eyes seemed heavy. I think this whole situation had taken its toll on both of us.

"It's not your fault." I sighed. "Maybe Nikki will get distracted between now and getting home. But I won't hold my breath," I quickly added.

I know my sister. As soon as I opened the apartment door, she was standing there with her arms folded across her chest, a smug look on her face. My mother was sitting on the living room sofa. The glare in her eyes left no doubt that Nikki had made good on her threat.

"Sit down," my mother commanded before I even closed the door all the way.

"Mom, let me explain," I began.

"Sit down," she repeated forcefully.

I huffed as I sat down.

"Where have you been?" she asked.

"Nowhere. I was just out chillin'."

"Nowhere, huh? Would nowhere be somewhere with that boy?"

"Mama, I don't understand. You liked him before all this happened. Now you act like he's the worst boy in the world. And it's not even his fault. He's just as sick about what happened as we are. He has no control over what his brother does."

My mother quickly tapped her foot, a nervous habit she had whenever she was trying to stay calm. "I didn't say he did. But I am saying, as your mother, I don't want you talking to him. I thought I made that clear."

"So we both gotta be punished for something his brother did?" I asked.

"Jasmine, baby, you have to understand your mother's position." I turned toward my grandmother. I hadn't even realized that she was in the room. She was leaned up against the doorway. She wiped her hands on her apron as she walked over and sat down next to me. "The memories. The pain. It's all too fresh. Your brother hasn't even been gone two months. And the thought of you with anyone who was connected to the boy responsible for Jaquan not being with us is just too painful right now."

I looked around the room as my mom and sister nodded in agreement. "Well, when will everybody be okay with it? How much time has to pass?" I asked.

"We'll never be okay with it," my mom snapped.

My grandmother shot her a chastising look.

"This just isn't fair," I muttered.

"Life ain't fair," Nikki interjected. "This is just sad. Don't you care nothing about your brother?"

"Shut up. Ain't nobody talking to you!" I spat.

"Let us handle this, please," my grandmother said to Nikki. She rolled her eyes.

"All I know is, if somebody I knew was responsible for killin' my brother, I wouldn't have nothin' to do with him." She wiggled her neck, rolled her eyes, and stormed down the hallway.

My mother and grandmother continued talking, but I didn't hear them. I'd tuned them out as I tried to figure out what in the world I was going to do now.

23

Angel

Alexis really did think she was Beyoncé. We were all in my living room, lazily lying around while Angelica slept in the back room.

Alexis was trying to copy the moves from Beyoncé's "Irreplaceable" video.

"To the left, to the left, everything you own is in the box to the left," she sang.

"To the no, to the no," Camille replied, waving her hand. "Any talent you had went out the doo'."

Jasmine and I cracked up laughing. It was good to see Jasmine laughing for a change. Between all this drama with her family not wanting her to see C.J. and her still grieving over her brother, she was in a foul mood all of the time. It had taken all our best efforts just to get her to come over today.

"Here," Alexis said, passing Camille her bottle of Cool Blue Gatorade.

"What's that for?" Camille asked.

"Since you drinking haterade, I just thought I'd help you out," Alexis replied.

Camille cut her eyes.

"And the award for Corniest Person on the Face of the Earth goes to . . . Alexis Logan!" Jasmine exclaimed.

Again we all laughed.

"Whatever." Alexis giggled as she went back to singing.

"When is the pizza coming?" Camille asked. "I'm starving."

I eyed the clock. "It should be here any minute. It's been an hour." Just then the doorbell rang. "That's probably the pizza man now."

My stomach was already growling as I thought about the thick-crust pepperoni pizza. I threw open the front door and *so* could not believe my eyes. Standing on my doorstep was the last person I ever expected to see.

"Marcus? What are you doing here?" I said.

"Hey, Angel. What's going on?" He looked scared and nervous.

Before I could respond, Camille appeared at the door next to me.

"Yeah, Marcus. What are you doing here?" Camille sneered. I'd told my girls about the way he'd acted the day I dropped by his house and when I'd called him, so needless to say, they had no love for him.

Marcus ignored Camille. "I came to see my daughter."

"Oh, so now you have a daughter?" Jasmine said, she and Alexis both appearing on the other side of me.

Marcus rolled his eyes as he kept his attention on me. "Can you call off your bodyguards and go get Angelica?"

I was still too stunned to speak. Luckily, I didn't have to. "Unh-unh. Angelica don't know you," Camille said, wagging her finger.

"And we ain't about to go get her, push her in front of some stranger, and say, here's your daddy," Alexis added.

"Yeah," Jasmine echoed. "I don't know who you think you are just waltzing up in here like you daddy of the year."

"First of all, I am her daddy." He grimaced, like it hurt him to say that.

"Oh, really? You're her daddy now?" Camille said. "It took you a year and a half to realize that?"

"Second of all, mind ya business. Angel, again, can I talk to you? Just you?" I couldn't believe this. When we'd talked last, Marcus had showed no signs that I'd gotten through to him. "I won't take long. So can I talk to you?" he repeated.

"Naw," Camille said. "You can't."

I shook off my shock. It was cute how my girls were coming to my defense, but I really needed to find out what he wanted. "It's all right."

All three of them shot me looks like I was crazy.

"No, seriously, it's cool. I need to hear this." I eased out the door. "Just chill. I'm sure it won't take long."

They groaned but backed off as I stepped out onto the front porch. "I'm listening," I said.

"Look, I know I ain't been around much—"

"Much? Try at all," I said, still trying to figure out where he was going with this.

He shifted nervously. "It's just I wasn't ready for no kid. I mean, I'm only seventeen."

"And you think I'm ready? I'm sixteen. Do you think I wanted to be a mother? No, but I made my bed and I had to lie in it. You, on the other hand, just jetted." It felt good to be finally giving him a piece of my mind. The few times we talked, I didn't really go off like I wanted to.

"While you out chillin' and runnin' the streets, I'm here taking care of Angelica by myself," I continued.

He lowered his eyes. *Was that shame I saw on his face?*

"Look," I said, my harsh tone softening, "why don't you tell me why you're here? Because a couple of weeks ago, you wouldn't even claim my baby. Now you're talking about 'your daughter.' "

"It's my mom. Your visit the other day really got to her. Sh-she's sick and she wants a relationship with Angelica, before something, you know . . . in case something happens to her."

I stared at Marcus. He no longer seemed like the hard, doggish guy who had played me for a fool. He seemed, I don't know, real. Still, I wasn't about to let him use my baby.

"Marcus, Angelica isn't some get-better-soon doll."

"I know that. And I know you don't owe me nothing,

but it would mean a lot to my mom if you would let her meet Angelica."

"So you came here because your mom made you?" I asked.

"No. I mean, yeah, I'm trying to honor her wish and let her see the baby."

"*Our* baby is not a *baby* anymore."

He paused. "And the stuff you said on the phone, it hurt. I mean, my dad bounced on me and I grew up hating him. And I . . . I guess I don't want Angelica to hate me. So, please, can I see her? It would mean a lot to me. And," Marcus continued, shifting uncomfortably, "I made my mom a promise that I would try to do right by Angelica. I know you think I just wanted to forget she even existed, and in a way, I did. I wasn't ready to face my mistake. I was scared. I wasn't ready for what a baby could do to my life."

"And so now you are?"

"No," he said pointedly. "But I realized I don't have a choice about it. She deserves to know me and my family. And any problems I have, I just gotta get over."

I hesitated with my arms folded across my chest. "That's all I've ever wanted." I glanced back toward the front door. As expected, Camille, Jasmine, and Alexis were peering out the front window.

I let out a deep breath. "Look, why don't you come back tomorrow? That way my girls will be gone and you can meet your daughter . . . for the first time," I couldn't help adding. "And I need to talk to my mom, and maybe, if everything goes well, we can take her to meet your mother."

I knew my mother was so religious that she was going to urge me to forgive Marcus and his mother. But me, I wasn't so sure. Miss Rachel was always teaching forgiveness, but I was going to have to pray hard on this one.

"Okay, I'll see you tomorrow. Around the same time?"

I nodded reluctantly. What was I doing? And would it be something I'd live to regret?

Marcus shot me a tight smile before he turned and headed back to his car. I took a deep breath, pushed open the front door, and braced myself to hear my girls' mouths.

24

Jasmine

I pulled another trash bag out of the box and walked back over to Camille, Angel, and Alexis. They were with two other girls from our school picking up trash in Hermann Park.

There were about seventy-five teens in all taking part in the citywide cleanup day. Of course, I would have rather been doing anything other than picking up trash. But Miss Rachel was adamant that we "give back to the community" on a regular basis. She was always saying we'd been so blessed in our lives that it was our duty to be a blessing to others.

I didn't feel blessed right about now, though. I'd been banned from seeing the love of my life. We were reading

Romeo and Juliet in my English class. I could so relate to their story because I felt like a ghetto Juliet who couldn't see her Romeo because their families didn't like each other. Only I dang sure wasn't about to kill myself. I loved C.J. and all, but I sure didn't want to die.

"Would you stop standing there daydreaming?" Rachel said. "You've over here in your own world and Camille's busy flirting with the football players from Worthing High School. I swear that girl forever has boys on the brain."

Miss Rachel handed me another trash bag. "Go over there and take this to Camille and tell her I said to get to work."

"Yes, Miss Rachel," I said, smiling.

I headed across the park to where Camille was standing in a crowd of boys batting her eyelashes. If she only knew how stupid she looked, I thought.

I was just about to call out to her when some guy trying to catch a football bumped right into me, knocking me down.

"Would you watch what you're doing?" I snapped.

"My bad," he said, reaching down to help me up. "Oh, what's up, foxy mama?" It was Tonio.

I snatched my hand away and stood up on my own. "I told you, I ain't no foxy mama," I said, wiping my pants off.

He smiled. I think he was trying to look sexy. But his gold teeth just didn't do it for me.

"It's Jasmine, ain't it?" he said.

"No, actually, it's none of your business." I looked at him with disgust before turning and walking off.

"Sorry to hear 'bout your brother!" he called out after me. That caused me to stop dead in my tracks. I slowly turned around.

"Doggone shame the way your man's kinfolk took him out. I guess he had to learn the hard way 'bout messin' with the wrong dude." Tonio stood licking his lips and looking cocky.

My chest heaved as I tried to calm myself. Camille must've heard him and seen me about to lose it because she came racing over just as I started heading toward him. Gang or no gang, it was about to be on.

Camille jumped in front of me. "Jasmine, no! Don't do this." She put her hand on my chest. "This boy is dangerous," she whispered.

I was trying to catch my breath and keep the tears at bay, but his taunting wasn't making it any easier.

"See, if your brother had gotten with us, maybe our *little* gang could've protected him."

"You probably put Al up to it!" I yelled, lunging at him.

Camille was no match for my strength and I easily knocked her to the ground as I charged at him. This time it was Miss Rachel who stopped me. I don't even know where she came from, but suddenly she had me by the arm and was pulling me back.

"Jasmine! I can't believe you!" she said.

I could no longer hold back the tears. "But, Miss Rachel—"

"But nothing. We've made so much progress in controlling your temper. You cannot do this." She leaned in closer to my ear. "And you definitely can't do this with him."

Tonio was standing there grinning like the whole thing was funny to him. Reality quickly set in. Miss Rachel was right. What in the world was I thinking? I knew that boy didn't fight fair. There was no telling what he had underneath that black jacket.

"Young man, why are you out here?" Rachel asked, turning around to face him but keeping her hand gripped firmly on my arm.

"Me and my boys just playing a little football. This is a public park, ain't it?"

By this point a crowd had stopped working and were staring at us. Tonio was just about to say something else when he glanced over and saw two Houston police officers heading our way.

"But we were done, so we're gonna let you all get back to picking up the trash." He motioned to his boys and they quickly made their exit.

I rubbed my temple in frustration. Miss Rachel patted my back.

"It's goin' to be okay, Jasmine."

I looked at her skeptically. All I could think was, Will the drama ever end?

25

Angel

I pushed another load of dirty laundry down into the washing machine. After pouring in the baby-safe detergent, I moved over to the dryer, where I took out the load of whites that had just finished drying.

Have I said it before? Being a teenage mom ain't no joke. I think I was feeling sorry for myself because, once again, my girls were out kickin' it—this time at Willowridge High School's step show—and I was at home doing baby laundry. And with Angelica messing up two to three outfits a day, there was plenty of laundry to be done. Marcus had come by two days ago. I didn't tell Angelica who he was, but I let her play with him for about an hour. As I'd expected, my mom was all for letting Marcus and his mom be a part of Angelica's life. Honestly, I think I was so okay with the idea because I desperately needed help.

"*Angel, necesitas cerciorarse de tomar todas esas botellas fuera del lavaplatos,*" my mother said, walking in the room dressed in her church clothes.

"English, *Mami*, speak English," I said, a little bit more forcefully than I should have.

"As long as I pay the bills around here, I'll speak what I want," she gently said. "But you need to make sure and take all of those bottles out of the dishwasher," she repeated. "There. Is that better? Just because you're not around Spanish-speaking people, don't forget your roots, *mija.*"

I sighed as I picked up the basket. "I'm sorry, Mama. I didn't mean to sound rude."

She reached out and patted my face. "I know, sweetie. I also know that you're upset about not being able to go with your friends tonight. But I have church tonight, and Angelica has a cold, so she doesn't need to be going out to a sitter. And remember, she's your responsibility, not mine."

I know, you only tell me that every other day, I thought. Instead I just said, "Okay, Mama."

After seeing my mother out the door, I plopped down on the sofa, turned on the TV to watch *My Super Sweet 16,* and began folding clothes.

I had just started wondering how my girls were enjoying the step show when my doorbell rang. "What did Mama forget now?" I mumbled as I stood up. My mother was always forgetting something. I assumed it was her keys since she was ringing the doorbell.

I swung the door open. "Okay, what did you—" I stopped midsentence as I saw Marcus standing on my doorstep. He was grinning as he held a giant teddy bear in his arm.

"What's up, Angel?"

"Marcus. What's going on?"

"Ummm, nothing much. I, um, I just wanted to bring this by for Angelica." He held out the bear.

To say I was shocked was an understatement. I know Marcus had said he'd do better, but I never really expected him to stay true to his word.

"Well, are you gonna let me in?" he finally asked.

"Oh," I said, snapping out of my daze. "Yeah, come on in." He followed me inside. "Angelica is asleep, but if you want, I can wake her up. She has a cold and I was trying to let her rest."

"Nah, don't wake her. Just give her this." He set the bear down on the table. "What?" he asked when he noticed me standing there, staring.

"I'm just trippin', that's all. You know, a month ago, you didn't want to have anything to do with me or our daughter."

"Look, Angel," he said, a sad expression crossing his face. "I'm sorry again. But I never thought I would get along so well with Angelica. And I told you, I just got to thinking about things, and well, I want her to know me. Besides, my mom can't stop talking about her. I think visiting with Angelica has made her feel better already." He swallowed hard. "I know that what I did, you know, denying you and the baby and all, was pretty jacked up."

"You think?" I couldn't help saying.

He looked at me like he wanted me to shut up and let him finish. "But I'm tryin' to do right now, a'ight? Can we just not fight?"

I folded my arms. "Okay, fine."

We stood in an uncomfortable silence before he glanced over at the TV. "Hey, they're showing the rerun of Shaq's house on *MTV Cribs*," he said, noticing the "coming up next" commercial. "You mind if I stay and watch it? I miss it every time they show it."

I definitely didn't know how to answer that. Allowing him back into Angelica's life was one thing. Sitting up in my house, chillin' with him was another thing entirely.

"Come on," he said. "I'm not going to do anything to you."

I hesitated. Marcus was a jerk with a capital J, but he wasn't dangerous or anything. And I knew I definitely didn't want to get back with him, so I didn't have to worry about anything happening. Besides, like my mom said, I'm guarding my gift. "Whatever."

He flashed a smile, then sat down on the love seat. I sat back down on the sofa and returned to folding clothes. We actually watched two episodes of *MTV Cribs*, then sat up and laughed and talked for another thirty minutes. I eyed the clock. My mom would be coming home from church any minute, and she definitely wouldn't like me sitting up in her house with a boy, even if he was Angelica's father.

"I'm surprised I'm saying this, but I enjoyed talking to you," I said, standing up. "But you're gonna have to go before my mom gets back."

He stood as well. "Cool."

"Are you sure you don't want me to wake Angelica?"

"Naw, just give her the bear, and if it's okay with you, I'll come back and see her this weekend."

I nodded, still shocked. This wasn't some fluke. He actually was going to start trying to be in my daughter's life.

"Hey, I heard about what happened to your friend, Jasmine's brother. I'm sorry about that," Marcus said as I walked him to the door.

"Yeah, it's pretty messed up," I replied. "But even though Al is out on bail, I think they're gonna give him some serious time."

Marcus shook his head in pity. "He's a better dude than me. Gang or no gang, I just don't know if I could go down for something someone else did."

That stopped me dead in my tracks. "Excuse me? What did you just say?"

He flashed me a confused look. "What?"

"The part about going down for something someone else did? I mean, Al is the one who shot Jaquan."

He frowned up. "No, he's not."

"What? What are you talking about? The police arrested him and everything."

"And? They arrested the wrong person. Al was there, but he didn't shoot anybody. This guy named Tonio shot Jaquan."

My mouth fell open. "What?" I repeated. "How do you know that?"

He shrugged. "My boy was there. He was on the basketball court when it happened. So were a lot of other people."

"That's crazy. And if Al didn't do it, why wouldn't he tell police that?"

"I don't know." Marcus looked like he didn't know why I was asking him all these questions. "The whole snitching thing I guess. Like I said, he's better than me, because I'd be singing like I was Chris Brown."

"Well, if other people saw it, why didn't anyone come forward?"

"And have Tonio come gunnin' for them next? I don't think so." He must have noticed the expression on my face because he said, "And I would advise you to stay out of it. Tonio and the Blood Brothers ain't no joke. They ain't got no kind of conscience."

I heard what he was saying, but there was no way I wasn't going to tell Jasmine this, especially after withholding what I'd known in the first place. Not only could it free Al, but it could be just what Jasmine and C.J. needed to get their relationship back on track.

26

Jasmine

"He didn't do it!" Angel screamed into my ear after I said hello. I had been lying on my bed thinking about C.J. and this entire situation, trying to figure out how I could get my mom to see this wasn't his fault. I was still grounded for lying about going out with C.J., and it was looking more and more like there was no way we'd ever work this out.

"What are you talking about, Angel?" I sighed heavily. "Who didn't do what?"

"Al. He didn't shoot your brother. You have to tell C.J."

That made me sit up. "*What?* How do you know he didn't do it?"

"Marcus just left my house and he said that one of his friends was there and saw the whole thing. *Él no lo hizo.*"

Angel seemed so excited that she was rambling and had started speaking half in English and half in Spanish, which she did often when she got nervous or excited.

"Wait. Slow down, Angel. You know I can't understand you when you start speaking Spanish," I said in frustration. "And did you say what I think you said? Why was Marcus at your house?"

"That's not important right now. I'll tell you about that later." Angel calmed down before continuing. "Al didn't do it. Marcus told me that Tonio is the one that actually pulled the trigger; not Al. Al is just taking the blame for it. Something about not wanting to be a snitch."

I was too stunned to talk. A million thoughts were racing through my head. Did I call C.J. and ask him about it, or did I go tell my family the news? I was so deep in thought that I almost forgot Angel was on the phone. She had been rambling on the whole time I was lost in thought.

"Jasmine, Jasmine! Are you listening to me?" Angel was yelling into the phone.

"Yeah, girl. I'm here. I need a big favor. I'm not supposed to talk to C.J. anymore. My mom is still trippin'. I shouldn't even be on the phone right now. Can you call C.J. and ask him to meet me at your house in twenty minutes?" I said as I tried to think of a way to get out of the house since I had been sentenced to my room for a month.

Angel must have been reading my mind. "How are you going to get out of the house? Aren't you grounded?" she asked.

"Don't worry about that. I'll think of something. I'll say I have a Good Girlz project or whatever. She'll let me out for that."

Thirty minutes later I was walking up to Angel's house. I had told my mom that the Good Girlz had a service project at the Hester House and we were all meeting at Angel's. Nikki had reluctantly dropped me off. I actually felt bad about lying to my mother, but desperate times called for desperate measures. Nikki had just pulled away when C.J. pulled up and parked in front of Angel's house. My heart was pounding as I nervously waited for him to bring the car to a stop.

"Hey." C.J. smiled as he rolled down his window. "This must be pretty important if you are risking a beat-down from your mom by sneaking out to see me."

"Yeah, it's pretty important," I responded as I got in on the passenger side. "We really need to talk. Where is your brother right now?"

C.J. cocked his head to the side and got a confused look on his face. "He's at home. My parents won't let him leave the house at all. Why are you asking about him?"

"I got some information today that I think we need to go and talk to him about. Has he said anything to you about what happened that day?" I questioned.

"Naw, he won't really talk about it. Just says that it never should have happened."

"He won't talk about it because he didn't do it, C.J."

C.J. closed his eyes and put his head back on the headrest. "Jasmine, what are you talking about?"

"Angel told me that she talked to her baby's father, Marcus, today and he says that Al didn't do it. A friend of his was there and saw everything." I looked over at C.J. I could tell he was shocked.

"Someone else at school said that, too. But when I asked Al, he told me to just accept that he did it," C.J. said, shaking his head.

It was my turn to be confused. "But why would he say he did it if he didn't?"

C.J. shrugged. "I don't know, but if it's true, that will make everything so much better. It won't bring Jaquan back, but at least both our families will be at peace knowing who really killed him." C.J. blew out a frustrated breath. "But I'm with you. If he didn't do it, then why would he take the blame for it?"

"I don't know, but I say we go talk to him and find out the truth. I know he'll talk to you if you ask him straight out," I suggested.

C.J. agreed and we drove to his house in silence. Once we got there, we were both relieved to see that neither of his parents were home. We knew Al would be more open without his parents there. C.J. unlocked the door and walked quickly into his brother's room.

"Say, Al, we need to talk," he said to his brother, who was lying across his bed with a pillow over his head.

"C.J., what's up?" Al said as he sat up. His eyes grew wide at the sight of me. "Jasmine. Wh-what are you doing here? How's your family doing? Look," he continued, not giving me time to answer, "I wanted to say something in court, but your moms was looking like she wanted to kill me. I'm so sorry. Can you tell her that?"

I nodded. C.J. let out an exasperated sigh. I could tell he was upset. "Al, I'm going to get straight to the point, and I am only going to ask you this once, so I want the truth. Did you do it?"

Al looked shocked for a minute, then tried to put on a tough front. "Dawg, why you coming at me like that? You trippin'." He flipped over and laid back down on the bed.

C.J. pulled his leg. Al jerked it away. "Would you quit? Leave me alone 'fore I bust you in your jaw," Al snapped.

C.J. pulled his leg again. "Man, take that hard-core act to somebody who doesn't know you. Get up and talk to me. Or I'll go get Daddy and let you talk to *him*."

That got Al's attention, because he turned back over and sat up. He let out a long sigh and I know I saw tears in his eyes.

"I know you didn't do it," C.J. said. "Who did?"

"It was Tonio," he finally said.

"What!" C.J. exclaimed. "Al, why would you not say something? That's crazy." C.J. sat down next to him. "I don't understand. You're facing some serious time."

Al started nervously wringing his hands. He looked so sad and pitiful. His eyes were puffy and had dark circles underneath them like he hadn't slept in days. After sitting quietly for a few moments, he began to tell us what really happened that day.

"I had the gun," he began. "Tonio just wouldn't let up.

He told me I had to prove my loyalty if I wanted to be a Blood Brother. Then . . . then he started threatening me. So, I told myself I was just gonna shoot and miss; pretend I had bad aim. But when we got to the basketball court, I couldn't even point the gun."

He looked at me like he was begging me to believe him. "I'm not a killer. I told Tonio I wasn't gon' do it. He snatched the gun from me, called me a punk, and fired two times. Jaquan's back was to us, so he never saw it coming. Both bullets hit him. Tonio dropped the gun and took off running. There was so much commotion. I didn't know what to do, so I ran, too. It all happened so fast."

By this point, all three of us were crying. I was crying for my brother, and I know C.J. was crying for his.

"Tonio told me I better not say anything, or me and my family would be next. I was scared and didn't know what else to do, so I just didn't say anything. I didn't want to be a snitch, but more than anything, I couldn't let anything happen to my family," Al sobbed.

C.J. wiped his eyes and looked at his brother. "Al, why would you want to be in a gang?"

"C.J., you just don't understand. Everybody, from Mama on, is always punking me and giving me a hard time. I just thought . . . being with the Blood Brothers would make people respect me."

C.J. looked like he wanted to chastise his brother some more, but the tears streaming down Al's face must've stopped him because he said, "Regardless, you cannot go to jail for the rest of your life for something that you didn't do. You have to tell the police."

"No way," Al said, quickly wiping his eyes. "Did you just hear me say Tonio said I'd be next? And he wouldn't hesitate to hurt you, Mama, or Cynthia."

"Fool, you could be next, even if you end up in jail. This is serious. There has to be something that we can do," C.J. said.

"No!" Al exclaimed. "C.J., man, I'm serious. Let me handle this."

C.J. stood up. "No. I let you handle this your way and look at what happened. Now we're gonna handle it my way."

C.J. grabbed my hand and led me out of the room. I had no idea what he had planned, but I was scared to death.

27

Jasmine

I was still clueless about what C.J. had up his sleeve. All I knew was that he'd asked me to call Miss Rachel and see if she was available to talk to us. She was, but she had 101 questions, none of which I could answer. Finally she agreed to meet with us that afternoon.

"Nikki, have you seen my black headband?" I asked my sister as I searched all over the top of our dresser, where I was sure I'd left it.

"Nikki?" I repeated when she didn't answer. "I know it was up here. I wish y'all would just leave my stuff alone." I spun around to continue my tirade against my sister, who was still nestled under the covers of her twin bed.

I could have sworn I heard sniffling, so I stopped going

off. "Nikki?" I said, easing toward her bed. When I got to the head of her bed, I saw that she had a picture of Jaquan clutched to her chest. "Are you okay?"

She shook her head. "I just miss him so much," she said, sniffling. "I know y'all think I'm a witch, but Jaquan didn't. He was the only one who believed in me, and he used to tell me I should go to community college. He always told me I was better than working in a beauty supply store. When I was sad about Tony breaking up with me, he told me, don't worry." Tony was Nikki's ex-boyfriend, who everybody thought was going to go pro in basketball. Nikki had thought he was gonna be her ticket to the good life, and she'd put up with a lot from him. But he'd dumped her last year. She shouldn't have been too upset though, because last I heard he was working at Pep Boys.

Nikki sat up in bed just as I sat down on the edge. "I was so sad about Tony, and Jaquan wiped my tears and told me he was gonna go pro, and he would take care of me, so I didn't have to depend on some random dude. He said as soon as he made it pro, the first thing he was gonna do was pay for me to go to fashion design school."

I had to bite my bottom lip to keep from busting out laughing at that. Nikki, a fashion designer? Oh, yeah, right.

Nikki fingered his photo. "Now what am I gonna do?"

The whole scene was a little shocking to me. Number one, I'd never seen my sister so sad, and number two, we'd never shared a sensitive moment like this.

"Ummm, Nikki, Jaquan was right. You can do better," I said. "You can go to Houston Community College, or even, ummm, even, ummm, fashion design school," I managed to add.

She eyed me skeptically. "I know you don't believe me, but I loved Jaquan so much. That's why I can't understand why you'd want to have anything to do with anybody remotely close to his killer."

I paused. I desperately wanted to tell her the truth about Al. But C.J. had sworn me to secrecy until after we talked to Miss Rachel.

"Nikki," I said, standing up. "I need you to trust me, just for a minute. Tomorrow, I think things will get just a little better for us."

She flashed me a confused look. I decided to get out of there before she pressured me to explain. I was supposed to meet C.J. at the corner store in a few minutes anyway.

"Look, I gotta go. Please just tell Mama I had to run over to Camille's. But only if she asks."

"Jasmine, where are you going?"

I backed up toward the door. "Just trust me, okay? I'll explain everything tomorrow."

I eased out the door, down the hallway, and out the front door, hoping that for once my sister wouldn't be a jerk and would let me try to work everything out.

28

Jasmine

"Okay, I was getting worried," C.J. said as I slid into the passenger seat of his car.

"Sorry I'm late, but I was talking to my sister." I was out of breath because I had sprinted all the way to the corner store.

"She's not giving you a hard time, is she?" C.J. asked, brushing a strand of hair out of my face.

"Naw. But I can't wait until I can tell her who really shot Jaquan. It's not like it'll even matter to her"—I looked at C.J.—"but it matters a lot to me."

He gave me a thin smile. "Me too. And you should be able to tell her when you get back home." C.J. threw the car in drive. "Come on, let's go."

As he pulled into traffic, I had to ask, "Can you tell me now why we're going to talk to Miss Rachel?"

"You're always talking about how cool she is and how much you trust her. That's what we need. Can you think of any other adult we can go to who can help us right now?"

I thought about it, then shook my head. My mom was too emotional, and she probably wouldn't even listen. His parents would race down to the police station, which I didn't see a problem with, but I could understand that Al was really scared something would happen to his family if the police got involved.

"I guess Miss Rachel is the only one who can help us," I said. "But what are you gonna ask her to do?"

"Well, you told me how she was friends with that lady down at the police station."

"Oh, yeah," I said, recalling Detective Lydia Patterson, who went to Miss Rachel's church. She'd saved our behinds when Alexis and I had gotten into trouble with shoplifting one time (long story). "Are you gonna ask Miss Rachel to call her?"

"I already have. They're supposed to meet us at the church," he said.

I leaned back in my seat, wondering how all of this was going to play out.

Ten minutes later we were standing outside Miss Rachel's office. C.J. squeezed my hand before knocking on her door.

"Come in," Rachel said.

I followed C.J. in. Miss Rachel was sitting behind her

large mahogany desk. Detective Patterson was in one of the plush leather chairs in front of the desk.

"C.J., Jasmine. Have a seat. Jasmine, you know Detective Patterson?"

I waved as I sat down.

"This is C.J., the young man I told you about," Rachel said. "Now, C.J., we both want to know what is going on. It took a lot of convincing to get Lydia here with the little information you gave me."

C.J. took a deep breath. "It's about Jaquan's shooting," he softly said.

Miss Rachel eyed me before turning her attention back to C.J. "What about it?"

"Al didn't do it, and we need to know what to do, because the boy who did do it is seriously threatening our family," he said after a brief hesitation.

"What do you mean your brother didn't do it?" Rachel asked, surprised.

"Apparently, this guy named Tonio, who is the leader of the Blood Brothers, tried to make Al shoot Jaquan as a sort of initiation. When Al wouldn't do it, Tonio grabbed the gun and fired." C.J. was now rushing his words out.

"My brother took the rap because Tonio told him he would kill me, my sister, and my mother if he didn't. That's why we have to handle this carefully. Al is scared that if Tonio is arrested, he or his boys will retaliate."

Rachel's hand went to her mouth. "Oh, my goodness." She looked at the detective. "What in the world can they do?"

"Well, I'm not handling that case," Detective Patterson

responded. "But when Rachel called me, I had a feeling this is what it was about, so I talked to the detective who is handling it. First of all, Al's fingerprints were on the gun."

"But I told you, he admitted that he handled it, he just didn't fire," C.J. said.

Detective Patterson held up her hand. "Let me finish. There was a second set of prints on the gun, and they belonged to Antonio Carver."

Relief washed over C.J.'s face. "See. There. Isn't that enough?"

The detective shook her head. "Actually, it's not."

C.J. looked defeated.

"But the statements we have from two eyewitnesses are," Detective Patterson continued.

"What?" C.J. and I said at the same time.

"I guess I can tell you, since Officer Carroll is making the arrest as we speak. We had two people come forward and provide statements that Mr. Carver was the trigger-man."

I was shocked. In my neighborhood, talking to the cops just didn't happen. People didn't want to get involved.

"I can't believe it," C.J. said.

"Believe it. We were a little shocked, too, but there are some good, well-meaning people in this day and age who want to see justice prevail. Couple those statements with our undercover officer, who has Tonio on tape bragging about the killing, and this should be open-and-shut."

"He was bragging about it?" Rachel asked.

"Young, stupid boys usually do. You'd be amazed at the

number of criminals who take pride in talking about their crimes. It just so happened that this doofus talked to an undercover officer from the mayor's Gang Taskforce. And this will be Antonio's third strike, so you can believe he'll be going away for a long time."

"Wow," was all I could say. I felt like I was living a movie. To think, we'd been all worked up, and the police had been on the case all along.

"So, you don't have to worry about Tonio blaming your brother. His own words will be his downfall." Detective Patterson stood. "Rachel, I need to get going. Glad I could be of help. C.J., you might want to get home. I think an officer is heading to your house to tell your family the good news. Now, just so you know, Al is probably going to get in a little trouble for brandishing a firearm and for obstruction of justice, but it'll be nothing like what he was facing before."

"Thank you so much!" C.J. exclaimed, hugging her.

"No problem." She waved as she left.

"Thank you, too, Miss Rachel." C.J. walked behind the desk and hugged her, too. "You just don't know how hard I've been praying that this would all work out."

"Prayer works," Rachel said with a smile.

"It sure does," C.J. said, coming back over to me and squeezing my hand. "It sure does."

29

Angel

I couldn't help staring at the hundred-dollar bill in my hand. I had to be dreaming. Had Marcus actually handed me some money?

"I know it's not much, but I just started working, so it's all I got," he said sheepishly.

I shook away my shock as I pushed the money down into my pocket. "Wow. Thanks. I really can use this."

We stood in an uncomfortable silence for a moment. "Well, is she ready?" he finally asked.

I inhaled deeply. Today was the first day I was letting Angelica go with him. It was his mother's birthday. Turns out, she had cancer and the only thing giving her joy was spending time with Angelica. Her family was having a birthday party at her house, and Marcus had begged me to let him come pick up Angelica and take her to the party.

Angelica still didn't know who he was. Right now, she called him Mr. Marcus. My mom and I knew we needed to tell her soon. But there was a part of me that just wanted to make sure Marcus was really goin' to stick around first.

"Yeah, let me get her." I walked to the back, and two minutes later returned with my daughter in tow. She was excited about going because she got to take her Elmo backpack. I half expected her to burst out crying when she realized I wasn't going with her, but she didn't. Instead, she just waved and sang, "Bye, Mommy."

A part of me was a little hurt as I watched Marcus strap her into the car seat. I wanted her to at least be a little sad about leaving me.

"It's going to be okay, *mija*," my mother said, appearing at my side.

I smiled through my tears. "It's funny, this is what I wanted, but I'm still a little sad."

"I know. But let's just thank God he finally came around." She leaned in and kissed my cheek. "I'm heading out to work. Your little friends are on the phone. What did you all do before conference calling?"

I smiled as I waved good-bye to Marcus and Angelica, then raced back into the house.

"Hello?" I said as I picked up the phone.

"Hey, girl," Camille sang. "It's us."

"What's up?" I asked, plopping down on the sofa.

"You tell us," Alexis said. "Did Marcus come get Angelica?"

"He did."

"What? You mean that buster actually showed up?" Jasmine scoffed.

"He did. And he gave me a hundred dollars."

"Get out of here," Jasmine said.

"A hundred dollars? What are you supposed to do with a hundred dollars? Shoot, a box of Pampers alone costs fifty," Alexis said.

"Pampers are not fifty dollars." I laughed. "A big box is about thirty."

"Fifty, thirty, what's the difference?" Alexis said. "He needs to come up with more than that."

"Yeah, tell him you need some back pay," Camille said.

I smiled. This was exactly why I didn't let them come over today, despite their whining and begging. I knew they would just give Marcus a hard time, and as much as I loved them, at the end of the day, he was still Angelica's father. So if he wanted a relationship with her, I wanted him to have it. I knew we'd never be together, but my daughter deserved a relationship with him.

"Can we change the subject?" I asked. "Jasmine, did you tell your family about Al yet?"

"I did. But it didn't seem to make much difference with my mom or my sister," she said dejectedly. "My mom listened, but she said it doesn't change anything—Jaquan is still gone."

"Oh, I'm sorry to hear that," I replied.

"I told her she should just give it time to sink in," Camille said.

"That's the same thing my grandma said," Jasmine replied. "In fact, the whole family has a counseling session with Reverened Adams, Miss Rachel's husband. Miss Rachel convinced my mom that we need to deal with our anger, then focus on forgiveness. She told me to just be patient and know that God was gonna work it all out."

"What happened to Al?" Alexis asked.

"They dropped the murder charge. He got sentenced to community service and was ordered to stay away from gangs. But C.J. said his family isn't taking any chances. They're sending Al to Iowa to live with his grandmother."

"Iowa, ewwww," Alexis said. "That's as bad as prison. Are there even any black people there?"

"I'm sure there are, Alexis," Jasmine replied. "Anyway, we start counseling next week, but in the meantime, me and C.J. still can't see each other. And I don't want to be sneaking around and lying, so we're just going to lay low for a minute."

"Girl, I couldn't stay away from my boo," Camille said.

"We know you couldn't, with your boy-crazy behind," Jasmine said. "And after all the trouble you got in with Keith, you'd think you would've learned your lesson. Not to mention Walter," she added, referring to the rich white boy Camille had dated against both her and his mothers' wishes. Then Walter, the son of a senator and a former beauty queen, was jumped by Keith. He was beat up so bad, he had to be hospitalized. Needless to say, Walter's mom went ballistic and made him stop seeing Camille.

"Okay, fine. I guess when you put it like that, it's not really worth it," Camille said with a groan.

"Miss Rachel would be proud to hear you say that," I said.

"Yeah, yeah, yeah," Camille said. "I guess I am learning a little from the Good Girlz. I even told Miss Rachel I was going to try to focus on my studies and leave boys alone for now, since she's always talking about how I have boys on the brain."

"I guess our goodness is rubbing off on you," I said.

"Oh, don't try to act like you're an angel, Angel." Camille chuckled.

"I don't know what you're talking about. I'm the sweetest one in the group," I said.

"Well, I'm the cutest," Alexis added. "And the smartest."

"I'm the flyest," Jasmine playfully chimed in. "And the baddest."

We all waited for Camille to throw in her two cents.

"What? Camille, you don't have anything to say?" Alexis asked.

"Camille?" I repeated.

"Huh? Oh, I had another call come in on my other line. I'm trying to see whose number it is. 281-799-74— Oh, snap, that's this cute boy I met at the mall yesterday! Hold on!"

She clicked over and left us in silence.

"Something is wrong with y'all's friend," Jasmine joked.

Camille clicked back over. "All right, ladies. Gotta go."

"Camille!" I chastised. "Didn't you just say you weren't going to focus on boys?"

"I said I was gonna *try* not to. But, girl, this boy is too cute. What?" she said after we didn't say anything. "It's all right. God is still working on me. Holla!"

We busted out laughing as my girl hung up the phone.

Readers Club Guide for

Friends 'Til the End

by ReShonda Tate Billingsley

Description

Jasmine, Angel, Camille, and Alexis are back for more fun, friendship . . . and drama. The Good Girlz have been through plenty of rocky times together, and they're about to face their toughest challenge yet. Jasmine is blissfully happy with her new boyfriend, C.J. But complications arise when a sudden tragedy threatens to tear both of their families apart. Meanwhile, Angel must cope with life as a single teenage mom while her baby's father refuses to provide help or even meet their child. The Good Girlz rely on faith, hope, and a little bit of humor as they learn about loss, love, and growing up.

Questions for Discussion

1. How does Billingsley foreshadow the tragedy that occurs midway through the novel?

2. Jasmine says, "I don't know how she does it, but Miss Rachel always has a way of getting me to do what she wants." (page 124) Why is Rachel so influential to the Good Girlz? How does she help them?

3. Angel's mother asks Angel, "[W]hy did you let Marcus talk you out of something worth so much more than this hundred-dollar bill?" (page 98) What does Angel's mother mean?

4. Why doesn't Angel tell Jasmine about the conversation she overheard between Al and his friend even after the shooting takes place?

5. What did you think about Angel's reaction to Marcus when he showed up at her house? Do you think she did the right thing?

6. Discuss the parallels between Jasmine's and C.J.'s families. How do their families influence their relationship?

7. What did you think about Jasmine still wanting to be with C.J. even when she thought Al was guilty? Did this surprise you?

8. How do the various characters respond differently to tragedy? Who handles it best?

9. Miss Rachel tells Jasmine, "Don't you know that everything that happens, happens for a reason?" (page 125) Do you agree with her? How might the painful events Jasmine and her friends experience influence them in a positive way in the future?

10. Discuss the themes of faith, hope, and love in the novel.

11. Several supporting characters, such as Nikki, Marcus, and Al, reveal a different and/or surprising side

of themselves over the course of the novel. What did you learn about each of them? Who surprised you the most?

12. How did each of the Good Girlz change by the novel's end? Who has matured most over the course of the Good Girlz series?

13. Do any of the situations in this book remind you of things that you and your friends have been through? How do you handle tough times?

14. Discuss the aspects of the novel that you liked most and least. What are some of your favorite scenes and quotes?

Activities to Enhance Your Book Club

1. Jasmine says her relationship with C.J. reminds her of *Romeo and Juliet*. Make some popcorn and watch one of the film versions of this classic story of star-crossed lovers.

2. Have a mother-daughter day with your book group. Get both generations together for manicures, a shopping trip, or dinner at a fun restaurant.

3. Check out www.volunteermatch.org or www.network forgood.org for ways that you can support programs working toward stopping gang violence.

4. For more information on ReShonda Tate Billingsley and the Good Girlz visit www.reshondatatebillingsley .com and www.myspace.com/goodgirlz1.

Don't miss the first book in this inspiring teen series

Nothing But Drama

Available in paperback from Pocket Books

Turn the page for a preview of *Nothing But Drama* . . .

Camille

I stood outside the small meeting room and checked out the girls inside. There were four other girls there besides me and Angel. One of them, a high yellow girl with a Beyoncé weave, was busy primping in the mirror. Then there was the weird-looking chick dressed in all black sitting in the corner. She looked like a serial killer.

Another girl was looking around nervously like she was scared to death that someone was about to steal her lunch money. Maybe she was scared of Jasmine, who sat two seats down from her. Jasmine's scowl was back and she looked like she would hit anybody who even looked at her the wrong way. She sat in a chair with her arms crossed and her legs gaped wide open like a guy. She looked like she really didn't want to be here.

"I know that feeling," I muttered.

"Did you say something?" Angel whispered. She was the only person who seemed halfway interested in being there.

I shook my head. "Nah, just ready to get this over with. Come on."

I walked into the room with Angel close on my heels. "What's up, y'all?" I was trying to be friendly to these losers as I sat down next to the scary girl.

Angel gave a meek wave and sat down next to me.

Jasmine didn't reply. Neither did Goth girl. Scary girl looked away and Miss Prissy kept flinging her hair.

"I guess these stuck-up girls are too good to speak," I told Angel loud enough for them to hear.

Jasmine sat up in her seat and dropped her arms like she was ready to rumble. "Who you calling stuck-up when you all up in other people's business?"

Now, I know I had just witnessed this girl beat the crap out of a guy, but for some reason I wasn't intimidated. Don't get me wrong, I'm definitely not a fighter, but I'm no punk, either. "If the shoe fits."

Jasmine stood up and started walking toward me. I kept my game face on but I couldn't help but think if she hit me, I was gon' have to grab something and try and knock her out because no way could I win a fistfight with her.

"Now, I know you two are not about to fight up here in the Lord's house."

We all turned toward Rachel, who had just stepped into the meeting room. No one answered her.

"Jasmine, you promised no fighting," Rachel said as she walked into the room. "I go into my office for one minute and walk back out here to find you all at each other's throats before you even know one another's names." Rachel walked to the front of the room and set her Bible and a folder down on the podium. "Rule number one: There will be absolutely no fighting in this church."

"Then you better tell this pint-size freak to leave me alone," Jasmine said as she glared at me.

I had my nerve back now that Rachel was in the room to keep me from getting killed. "I guess everybody would be pint-size to you, you—"

"Enough!" Rachel snapped.

"You better tell her, Miss Rachel," Jasmine said.

"I got this, Jasmine. Sit down." Rachel turned toward me. "You have a seat, too." She waited for both of us to sit back down. "Now, this is not the way I wanted us to get things started. We are in this for the long run, so we might as well all learn to get along." Rachel took a deep breath, then flashed a bright smile. "Let's start by introducing ourselves. I'll go first. Welcome to the first meeting of the Good Girlz. For those of you who don't know, I'm Rachel Adams. I'm the First Lady of Zion Hill and the founder of the Good Girlz. Don't let the name fool you. We're not trying to make you out to be Goody Two-shoes."

I tried not to smile. She must've been reading my mind.

Rachel continued. "But we do want to get you to realize that you are entitled to the good things in life. None of us here are better than anyone else. We all have issues and our goal is to help each other work through them. We'll also take part in some service activities and do our share of giving back to the community."

Rachel clapped her hands together. She was obviously excited about this program. "We will deal with your issues and discuss ways we can live more godly lives."

I couldn't help but let out a disgusted sigh. Here we go with the preaching.

"But first, let's start by just having everyone give their names. Then we'll come back and let you tell a little about yourself," Rachel continued.

Angel introduced herself first. Then me, then everybody else. The scary-looking girl was Sasha. Tameka was the girl dressed all in black like she was going to a funeral or something. And the diva over there was Alexis.

"Now, let's move on and talk about ourselves." Rachel smiled at us, but I wasn't taking the bait. "When I say we all have issues, I just want you to know that includes me. While I'm a proud First Lady now, and the daughter of a preacher, I ain't always been holy." She stopped and laughed, piquing my interest.

"Even now, it takes a lot of effort for me to walk the straight and narrow. I'm a preacher's kid . . . and you know what they say about preacher's kids."

"Y'all the worst ones," I offered. The other girls laughed along with me. Except for Jasmine. She still had a scowl.

"I don't know about all preachers' kids, but I can tell you this preacher's kid was pretty bad," Rachel said. "Any crazy thing you've done behind a boy, I've already done it. Any disappointment you might have given your parents, been there, done that. So I'm hoping you all will get to the point where you will feel comfortable opening up." Rachel turned toward me. "Your turn. What's your name?"

"Camille Harris."

"Okay, Camille Harris. Where are you from and what made you come here?"

The smile left my face. I didn't want to sit up in church and lie but I still wasn't feeling letting these girls all up in my business. "I'm from the southwest part of Houston. I go to Madison High School and I'm here, umm, because my mom thought it would be good for me."

Rachel looked at me like she knew there was more to the story. "Okay, I'm sure we'll get more in depth later."

I was grateful that she didn't push it and instead moved on to the scary-looking girl.

"And you would be?" Rachel asked.

The girl didn't respond.

"You don't have to be nervous," Rachel said.

She still didn't say anything.

"How about we come back to you?" The girl nodded and Rachel gave her a reassuring smile.

"Tameka, why don't you come out of the corner and come up here and introduce yourself."

Goth girl looked like she wanted to crawl up in a hole and die. She reluctantly moved toward the front of the room.

"My name is Tameka. I go to Hightower High School," she all but whispered.

"Tameka is my niece," Rachel said proudly. "She lives

in Missouri City, but she's here because I'm trying to expose her to different things, right?"

Tameka groaned, but didn't say anything.

"She's a little shy," Rachel said. "But we're going to work on that in this group. Right, Tameka?"

Tameka shrugged. Rachel sighed before turning her attention to Angel. "Your turn," Rachel said.

"Hi, I'm Angel. I attend Westbury High School, at least for now, anyway. I don't know if I'm going to stay there, because . . . things aren't going too good for me right now."

Rachel pressed on. "And why aren't things going well?"

Angel sighed. "I, um, I had to move away from my neighborhood."

"Where are your parents?" Alexis asked. I didn't even know she knew how to talk in complete sentences, since she hadn't bothered to say anything more than her name.

Angel looked real uncomfortable. "Me and my mom, well, it's just me." Angel puckered her lips together like she wanted to say more but she kept quiet.

"Oh, snap. I bet she's a runaway," Jasmine said.

"I am not a runaway," Angel protested. She shot Jasmine a mean look. "I'm staying with my sister right now."

"Whatever." Jasmine shrugged. "I just think you need to stop lying, that's all, especially all up in a church."

Angel glared at Jasmine like she couldn't stand her. "My mom didn't want me there. Does that make you feel better?" she snapped.

For once, Jasmine looked apologetic. "Dang, I'm sorry."

"I came here because stuff is tight with my sister and . . ." Angel dropped her hands in her lap and turned toward Rachel. "I was just hoping to win the drawing you were gon' have tonight because I really need the money." She looked like she was trying not to cry.

Rachel walked over to Angel and took her hands as she sat down next to her. "Angel, God doesn't do anything by chance. You are here tonight for a reason. He put that flyer in your hand. He led you here because He knew you need what this group can offer."

I tried not to turn up my nose. What could this group possibly offer besides wasting my time? Stop with all the negativity, this little voice in my head seemed to say. I turned my attention back to Rachel.

"Whatever demons you are wrestling with, we want to help you work them out." Rachel squeezed Angel's hand before standing up and walking back to the front of the room. "Part of our problem in trying to live a Godly life is that we don't know we're being attacked. Drugs, alcohol, whatever drives you away from a Godly life is a tool that the Devil uses to attack you."

I really was not trying to hear a sermon. I was tired and ready to get home. Rachel must've read the look on my face because she said, "And the Devil also messes with our mind so that we can't receive the Word when it's being fed to us." She smiled at me and I immediately felt embarrassed.

"Amen to that."

We all turned toward my mother, who stood in the meeting room doorway. She was wearing a gigantic smile.

"Can you tell them that again?" my mother said.

I couldn't help but groan as my mother walked into the room. She stuck her hand out toward Rachel. "I'm Mrs. Harris, Camille's mother."

Rachel shook her hand. "Nice to meet you."

"Sorry to interrupt, but Mrs. Washington said you'd be finished by seven," my mother said.

Rachel looked down at her watch. "Wow, I can't believe time has flown by that quickly." She looked at all of us. "We will wrap up for today but think on these two things. I want us to create a bond here and that means you all will communicate outside of the group. I want everyone to make sure your numbers are correct on this paper." Rachel handed a piece of paper to me. I reluctantly took it.

"I'll make copies for everyone and have them at the next meeting. I also need to give away that door prize I advertised," Rachel said.

Angel perked up.

"Normally, I would do a drawing," Rachel said. "But I want our first lesson of our group to be one of selflessness. How about we all agree to give it to Angel?"

Angel smiled as she nervously looked around.

"Anybody have a problem with that?" Rachel asked.

Me, Alexis, and Tameka shook our heads. Jasmine shrugged.

Before I knew it, I found myself saying, "I think that sounds like a good idea."

"Then it's a done deal." Rachel reached into her Bible and pulled out an envelope. She handed it to Angel. "I know you said you came for the money, but I hope you'll come back because you like being with us."

Angel blushed. "I will."

Rachel dismissed the group and we all headed for the door. Just a few minutes ago I was itching to get out of here, but as I looked at my mom standing in the doorway with that big stupid grin, I realized my two hours there weren't so bad after all.

Want more teen fiction fun?
Check out these titles:

Made in the USA
Coppell, TX
14 November 2021

65533004R00121